# A Young Man Is Gone

## Double-Twins Mystery #1

*Paul J. Kijinski, Jr.*

### By: Paul Kijinski
Award-Winning Author of *Camp Limestone*

12/16/2015

Copyright © 2015 Paul J. Kijinski, Sr.
All rights reserved.

*This is a work of fiction.* Names, characters, places, and
incidents either are products of the author's imagination or are
used fictitiously. Any resemblance to actual events or persons,
living or dead, is entirely coincidental.

ISBN: 1515239209
ISBN-13: 978-1515239208

# DEDICATION

*For my students in the South Euclid-Lyndhurst School District,
who have blessed me through the years with a wellspring of inspiration.*

# CONTENTS

# ACKNOWLEDGMENTS

Cover design by Cal Sharp at Caligraphics

The James Dean sketch on the cover was created in 2012 by Jon Attfield, who retains the copyright to that artwork. The image appears here under license.

Two other images on the cover are in the public domain, available through Wikimedia Commons:
- Minuteman III Launch Control.jpg (User: Chitrapa)
- NDAtlarge.gif (User: VitaleBaby)

The Beach Boys song "A Young Man Is Gone" (written by Bobby Troup) was originally released on their 1963 Capitol Records album, *Little Deuce Coupe*.

*******

Special thanks to Thomas Colombo, a young reader who devoured a draft of this novel in a single day and provided valuable feedback.

# CHAPTER ONE

House-sitting. The expression sounded pretty dumb to me when my father first mentioned it three months ago. All four of us—Mom, Dad, my sister Mandy, and I—were seated around the dining room table after supper. I asked, "What, are we supposed to go and just sit at someone's house for a whole month?"

"We'll look after things," my father replied. "You know, make sure nothing goes wrong with the place, plus cut the grass and tend the garden. Oh yeah, and keep little critters out of the house."

"Great," Mandy said sarcastically without taking her nose out of a book. "We'll put Mark in charge of the critters."

"No thanks," I said, "because that would include you."

Mandy turned a page and whisked her hand in the air toward me. I hate when she does that. Mandy is my twin sister. The two of us are usually pretty good friends, even though we don't have that much in common. She reads a lot—mostly mysteries or science fiction—while I spend as much time as possible hanging out with friends and playing sports. We're eleven years old, but because Mandy was born fifteen minutes ahead of me, she sometimes acts like she's the boss of our world. For example, one of her missions in life is trying to make me clean my room, and when I don't do it she reports to our parents just how messy it is. I think it's safe to say that most of our disagreements could be avoided if Mandy just minded her own business.

"Couldn't I stay here with Brandon?" I asked. "His parents would be totally fine with that."

"Sorry, Mark, but *your* parents wouldn't be fine with that at all," my mother said. "Dad and I couldn't go a month without you."

"Do I get to vote on that?" Mandy chimed in and actually looked away from her book for a moment. We were in the middle of one of our disagreement periods.

"Shut up," I growled at Mandy. Then I switched to my *pretty please* voice: "But Mom, I'm gonna miss my summer."

"You mean you're gonna miss your Sarah," my sister teased.

"Shut up," I growled again. I couldn't hit her, so I was saying "shut up" a lot.

"Knock it off with the shut-ups," Mom warned. "I'm getting real tired of that."

"Okay, okay," I said.

Mandy was right, though. I had a major crush on a girl named Sarah Beasley who goes to our school, and I wanted to spend time at the city pool trying to get her to like me back and become my first real girlfriend. House-sitting in North Dakota would mess up that plan. It would also mess up the plans I had made with my best friend, Brandon, and three other guys that we hang out with. Together we make up a pretty wicked street basketball team, and we were planning on entering summer tournaments.

The only person that Mandy would probably miss was her best friend, Gretchen. Mandy can be bad enough on her own, but when paired up with Gretchen, we're talking about the stuff of nightmares. In fact, I once had this dream where I was a patient in the hospital. I'm just minding my own business and slurping down Jell-O cubes, when suddenly Gretchen and Mandy enter the room and shut off the TV. They begin taking turns reading aloud to me from a Nancy Drew mystery. "Stop! No, please!" I'm yelling, but they go right on swapping paragraphs. I can't reach the Call button to get a nurse's attention, so I start slamming my head against the bed rail in the hopes of losing consciousness. . . . I actually woke up with a mega headache!

"Come on now, Mark. I'm asking for one month out of your whole life," my father reminded me. "Show some support for this crazy plan of mine. And who knows? It might even turn out to be an adventure for you. It's not every family that gets to live in an LCF."

Let me interpret my father's words here. His crazy plan was to spend the summer writing fiction, rather than earning extra money at the local Home Depot like he usually does. The reason he has summers off is that both he and my mom are teachers in Cleveland Heights, Ohio, the same city where we live. My dad teaches fourth grade, all subjects, and my mom teaches seventh-grade math. Mandy and I didn't go to our dad's elementary school, but we will wind up at my mom's school when we enter junior high this fall. That will be kind of creepy for me—being in the same building where my mom teaches—but I won't waste time worrying about that now. And at least both of my parents have a good reputation with kids, so that makes my life a little easier. Kids I don't even know come up to me all the time and say things like, "Hey, tell Mr. C. Tony says hi," or, "Tell Mrs. C. that Jamiya is taking AP Calculus next year." Almost all of their students say "C" because they have a difficult time pronouncing our last name, Cousineau—*koo-zi-no*. Anyway, my father has had a few short stories published in magazines over the years, but now he planned to work on a novel. He was sure that the peace and quiet in North Dakota would provide the perfect atmosphere for writing.

Now that brings me to the "LCF" part of my father's plan, which is where everything gets a whole lot crazier. An LCF is a Launch Control Facility, where an Air Force crew keeps track of giant nuclear missiles. If crews receive the proper commands, they would actually launch those missiles. Which would probably mean World War III. Which would probably mean the end of the world as we know it.

The LCF that we would be staying in is near Grand Forks, North Dakota, where my father served as a missile crewmember when he was in the Air Force. All fifteen of the LCFs belonging to Grand Forks Air Force Base were closed by the late 1990s—several years after the Cold War ended—and all of their missiles were shipped to another base somewhere in Montana. So, what do you do with multimillion-dollar LCFs once their mission is over? Well, the Air Force immediately turned one into a museum, but the rest remained empty until a few years ago. That's when the U.S. government decided to raise money by auctioning them off to the public.

As it turned out, one of my father's old Air Force buddies bought one. When my father left the Air Force and went into teaching, his friend Tommy Baxter started a software business and became a millionaire. He bought Foxtrot-Zero, his favorite LCF, just for old time's sake— just because he thought it would be cool to own a piece of military history. He and his family live in Seattle and spend only a few weeks out of the year at Foxtrot-Zero. That means the place is usually vacant, except when Tommy's old Air Force buddies decide to "house-sit" for him.

So, that's as much as I knew about my summer plans late last spring: that a few days after school ended, we would drive out to North Dakota and house-sit at a facility that had been built to defend the country with nuclear weapons; that I would miss out on my chance with Sarah; and that I would miss out on long days of b-ball and swimming with my friends.

"So what will I do for friends?" I asked my parents.

"That's one nice thing about being a twin," Mom assured me. "You always have each other."

"I said *friend*, not *freak*," I shot back. I know it's immature to say things like that, but sometimes I just can't help myself where my sister is concerned. Mandy was unfazed by my comment.

"That's enough," Dad scolded. "Mom will be heading to the university every day, so you can go with her and meet kids in town if you want to." Then Dad raised his eyebrows and lowered his voice a little, like he was about to tell us all a secret: "Plus, back at Foxtrot-Zero, there's always Bobby Swenson."

Dad got up from the table and carried our ice cream bowls to the dishwasher. A countertop and two overhead cabinets separate our dining room from the kitchen, so all we could see was the middle of Dad's body.

"Bobby who?" I asked.

"Oh George, don't start with that old story," Mom scoffed and shook her head.

"What story, Dad?" I asked. "What's Mom talking about?"

"Well, some people say Foxtrot-Zero is haunted by the ghost of a teenager named Bobby Swenson," Dad's disembodied voice replied.

"Yeah, right," I snorted.

"Did he die there?" Mandy asked seriously, putting down her book.

Dad suddenly ducked his head to the countertop level, holding a flashlight under his chin. "That's what they say," he hissed.

"Daddy!" Mandy exclaimed with joy at Dad's standard flashlight-shining-up-on-his-face trick. Sometimes Mandy acts like she's still four years old.

"Stop it, George!" Mom laughed. "And who's *they*? It's just a stupid story that crewmembers made up a long time ago when they had nothing better to do."

"Is that true, Daddy?" Mandy asked. I hate it when she calls him Daddy. It's just another sign of how she has him wrapped around her little finger.

Dad came back to the table without the stupid flashlight. "I can't say for sure, honey," he told Mandy. "But I did see some weird things when I was on duty at that site."

"Ooh, like what?" Mandy pounced. She was totally caught up in Dad's story now.

"Nothing huge. Just things like lights suddenly going off, and—"

"George, you're gonna scare these kids!" Mom interrupted. "And you're not exactly making our visit there sound too inviting."

"Not to worry," Dad said. "Strange things have happened only in the underground launch control center, and never in the aboveground house. You won't have any need to go down below anyway."

"Exactly," Mom concluded. "So don't give it another thought. I swear, crewmembers back in your father's day had a really warped sense of humor . . . and reality."

When both of our parents left the dining room, Mandy gave me her devilish half-grin, and I knew she was already hatching a plot in that mystery-twisted mind of hers. Something told me that her plot involved an underground launch control center and a ghostly teenager. And she would do her best to drag me into the mix.

"Hey Ma-ark," Mandy sang out, making two syllables of my name.

"Shut up," I snapped back before she could say another word.

"There's nothing to be afraid of, Ten-Point-Eight," Mandy replied with a taunting laugh and ran out of the room.

She knew better than to stick around after calling me Ten-Point-Eight. It's just a stupid nickname, but it got me mad. I was actually hoping that name would die out during the summer months, so maybe leaving town for a while would help move that process along.

Still, if we had to leave Cleveland Heights for a whole month, why couldn't we go someplace that normal families go, like Myrtle Beach, or Ocean City, or Orlando? In North Dakota, there would be no beaches or amusement parks to greet me; just long, dull days waiting to wrap their smothering arms around me. I was sure of it.

# CHAPTER TWO

News flash: Driving 1,062 miles in the sun for two days is no fun. My dad took the rear bench out of our minivan to allow for more cargo room, which meant that I had to sit right next to Mandy for the whole ride. From Ohio we traveled through Indiana, Illinois, Wisconsin, Minnesota, and finally into North Dakota. I listened to at least hundred songs on my iPod and read an entire book on chess. Some kids might think I'm a geek for liking chess, but it's really a cool game based on war strategies. My sixth-grade social studies teacher got me hooked on it.

When Mandy wasn't reading a mystery or a sci-fi thriller, she was writing in her journal. She picked up that habit from my father, who always jots down random ideas that he can later weave into stories. As we were passing through the Chicago area Mandy dozed off, and I couldn't resist borrowing her journal. It's not that I had any interest in reading what she'd written; instead, I had an urge to contribute to her work. I flipped to a clean page and wrote:

*Dear Journal,*

*I know it's not right to be jealous of people, but how can I help it when I live with Mark? Is it fair that he got the good looks, the charming personality, and the great mind? Sometimes I wonder if we're even twins at all. I don't feel worthy to consider him my brother, let alone my twin. This is why I like mysteries so much, because I want to find out where I really came from. Maybe Mommy and Daddy found me on—*

And that's as far as I got before the journal was snatched from my hands. I watched Mandy's eyes shift from left to right taking in my words, and I couldn't help but laugh. She pulled my hair hard, which hurt, so I flicked her ear. It made a satisfying *thunk* sound.

"Mom!" Mandy screamed, causing Dad to swerve outside our lane.

"What the –?" Dad yelled. "Don't you ever do that again!"

"Don't be mad at me, Daddy," Mandy pouted. "This idiot back here wrote something mean in my journal and then hit me in the ear! It's probably bleeding."

"It is *not* bleeding," I said.

My mother reached back from her front seat and smacked my arm. "Now you're hitting your sister? What's gotten into you?"

"I didn't hit her. I gave her a playful flick, but only after she pulled my hair. See, I guess she left that part out. Now who's the idiot?" I rubbed my arm as though I had been stung by a wasp. I was trying to work the guilt angle.

"Knock it off, the both of you," Dad yelled.

"But he stole my journal and—" Mandy began.

"I . . . said . . . knock . . . it . . . off," Dad warned through gritted teeth. He cranked up the radio volume.

When Dad talks through his teeth like that and inserts dramatic pauses between his words, Mandy and I know better than to say anything else. Mandy creased the page I'd written on and tore it out of her journal. She crumpled it and held it toward me.

"If you were my kid, I'd make you eat this," she said under her breath.

"If I were your kid, we'd both be eating our own puke," I whispered. "Just like all the other apes at the zoo."

Mandy whipped the crumpled paper at my head and I batted it away with my hand. And that's when it happened. The paper ricocheted off the front windshield and flew out the driver's side window, which my father had lowered about three inches. There was some amazing trigonometry going on at that moment, because there's no way Mandy and I could repeat that feat if we tried a thousand times.

You know those signs that say *Littering: $100 fine?* Well, they mean it. A Chicago police officer, who just happened to be driving right behind us, pulled us over.

"License and registration," the officer mumbled without even saying hello first.

Dad handed over the documents. "You know, officer," Dad began in a friendly tone, "that paper flew out of my window accidentally."

Mandy and I were as stiff as cadavers in the back seat.

"Sir, have you been drinking?" the officer asked.

"What? No, of course not," poor Dad replied.

"My husband has never even been pulled over before," Mom added with pride.

"Congratulations," the officer said, but he was not in a forgiving mood. He said he'd begun trailing us when he saw our van swerve, and that the littering incident had put the icing on the cake. *Ticket: $100.*

As our car merged back into traffic, Dad said to Mom through gritted teeth, "Cancel . . . the . . . Holidome."

Mom took out her cell phone and made a call. "Yes, I'm sorry too that we won't be staying with you," she said at the end of the conversation and looked back at Mandy and me with eyes that shot daggers into every vital organ of our young bodies. "And thank you for not charging a cancellation fee."

The best way to avoid any further trouble, I figured, was to be unconscious. I forced myself to sleep, and before I knew it we were pulling into the parking lot of a Super8 Motel in Madison, Wisconsin. I have to give my father credit for being an evil genius, because directly across the street from us was the Holidome where we would have been staying if only we were a hundred dollars richer. Holidomes provide an indoor swimming pool with slide, ping-pong tables, shuffle board, a cool restaurant, and a giant video game arcade. Super8s provide . . . a room and a crummy TV. We stood there in the hot parking lot, watching happy families enter the vacation palace across the street from us. One family of four, with brother and sister around five years old, actually locked arms and skipped across the parking lot to the Holidome lobby! Skipped—I'm not lying.

"Sweet family," Dad observed and handed me a suitcase.

"And the kids look to be the same age," Mom added. "They're probably twins."

So, instead of going nuts in the Holidome and maybe hanging out with some cool kids, I spent the evening reenacting famous chess matches on my traveling chess board. One of the chess books I had with me included entire matches, move by move. It's kind of weird because you can get into the minds of great players like Bobby Fischer and Boris Spassky, and think, *Hmm. Now I've got him hemmed in.*

One strange, non chess-related thought also crept into my mind: *Wouldn't it be cruel if Sarah Beasley is staying in the Holidome across the street from me right this second?* I realized that the odds would be about a gazillion to one, but I did know that she had relatives in Minnesota, and maybe she and her parents were on their way to visit them and decided to stop off in Madison. Maybe they were in the lobby when my mom called, and the desk clerk had said, "Mr. Beasley, you're in luck! Someone has just canceled their reservation." And that would mean Sarah was staying in *my* room, in a way. Cool. Even better, though, would be if both of our families had rooms in the same hallway.

If Sarah and I suddenly found each other staying at the same hotel, that would have been like Fate telling us that we were meant to be boyfriend and girlfriend. There's no other way you could interpret that situation! But I would never know. It's funny how something little—like a piece of crumpled paper—can make ripples in your life.

Just then I heard my dad snore. I looked around and noticed that everyone in the room was asleep except for me: Mom and Dad on one bed, and Mandy on the other. I was wide awake on the sofa pullout.

Instead of swimming with my new girlfriend, I'm sitting here playing both sides of a chess match that took place way before I was even born. You know something, Mark? You are a geek!

"Your move, Bobby," I said with a Russian accent to imitate Spassky.

"Did you say Bobby?" Mandy whispered. She was suddenly sitting straight up in bed. "Has he made contact with you?"

"Who?" I whispered back. "What are you talking about?"

"Bobby Swenson," she said seriously. "Gretchen and I did this little séance asking him to give us a sign. I thought maybe he came to *you* for some reason."

"Okay, look," I said. "If a dead teenager decides to contact me, I'll make sure the whole family knows about it right away."

"Why did you say 'Bobby' then?"

"I meant Bobby *Fischer* because I was in the middle of— Never mind. Just go back to sleep, Mandy. You're still dreaming."

"Whatever," she said and lay back down. At least she didn't whisk the air with her hand.

"Hey, good night," I said. Even though we get on each other's nerves, Mandy and I still have this unwritten rule where we're nice to each other right before going to bed.

"Good night," she replied.

# CHAPTER THREE

As we crossed the border into North Dakota the next day, my father was in a much better mood. He and my mom were both kind of giddy, which is a word that Mom uses to describe Mandy and her friend Gretchen after they've stayed up half the night reading out loud to each other.

"Hey, look—the Red River!" Dad announced happily. "Remember that time when we were down there filling sand bags before the flood?"

"How could I forget?" Mom said. "I was sore for a week."

"Oh, and all the sunflowers!" Dad cooed. "They're only a couple feet tall now, but just wait until you see how big they get while we're here."

"Wow," I said, rolling my eyes.

"They're beautiful, Daddy," Mandy said sweetly. *Suck up.*

I have to admit Dad was right about the sunflowers. In Cleveland Heights I was used to seeing a few of them here and there, dotting people's flowerbeds. In North Dakota, though, there were fields of them for as far as the eye could see. One of the country roads we drove on seemed to cut a tunnel through sunflowers, and we saw a teenage boy walking along the edge of that tunnel carrying a fishing rod.

"Must be a good pond somewhere back in there," Dad announced. He sounded as though he was making a mental note on where he himself could go fishing one of these days.

I tried to imagine what it would be like to live in such a rural place. I had always lived in a tightly packed neighborhood, where I could spit out my bedroom window and hit the next-door neighbor's house (*not that I would ever dream of actually doing that, Mrs. Haggerty!*). I imagined myself walking alone through a sunflower field. I had a weed dangling carelessly from my lips and a bamboo fishing pole jangling on my shoulder. Suddenly, I shuddered. I don't know why, exactly; I guess I just thought it would be creepy to be that alone—totally alone—in nature. Snakes and bears are one thing, but it also seemed to me that deep in nature would be the most likely setting for something supernatural to happen. And you can count me out where that stuff is concerned!

The town of Grand Forks, North Dakota, turned out to be bigger and nicer than what I'd expected. Dad said that about fifty thousand people lived there. As soon as we entered the town, we ate a late lunch at a restaurant called John Barleycorn's. Mom and Dad were thrilled that the restaurant was still there and that it still offered homemade croutons for their salads. *Homemade croutons? Big deal!* I was thinking. Once again, Mom and Dad were downright giddy.

"What you have to remember," Mom explained, "is that your father and I were newlyweds when we first lived in Grand Forks. We have a lot of great memories connected to this place."

After lunch we bought groceries and cruised around town. We looked at the campus of UND—University of North Dakota—where Mom finished her degree in teaching and where she would take graduate classes during the summer. We visited the Air Force base school where Mom did her student teaching. We saw the softball fields where both of my parents used to play on a coed team. And so on. I swear they had a story about every little thing they showed us.

Finally, I pointed to a bus stop. "Hey Dad, did you ever wait for a bus there?" I asked innocently.

"Hmm, I'm not sure," he replied, not catching my sarcasm.

"Or what about that nice pine tree over there, Mom?" I tried again. "Do you guys have any cool stories to tell us about that nice pine tree?"

"What? Oh, I get it," Mom laughed. "I think it's time for us to move on, George. We can relive more memories when we're on our own."

"I like hearing about your memories," Mandy chimed in.

"Mandy, why don't you just shu—" I began, and then remembered Mom and Dad's rule. "Shuck corn with me. Mom, do you want us to start shucking the corn now?"

"Great recovery, moron," Mandy baited me. And neither one of my parents said anything to correct her.

"Hey!" I protested. "How come it's okay for her to call me names?"

"Sorry," Mom replied. "We were so busy up here shucking corn, we didn't hear a thing."

*******

Dad held a pretend microphone to his lips as our van rolled up the access road to the Foxtrot-Zero LCF. "Foxtrot Control," he began, "this is Trip Eighteen-Dash-Six, now arriving your location. Request permission to enter."

"Roger that, Eighteen-Dash-Six," Dad replied to himself in a nasally Southern accent. "Y'all are cleared to enter."

Dad got out of the van and opened the lock on a wide gate that rested on wheels. He rolled the gate open, and as

Mom drove the van onto the site, Dad clicked off a smart salute.

"Oh, come on," I complained to Mom. "He's not gonna do that every time, is he?"

Foxtrot-Zero looked like a standard ranch-style home from the outside. It was painted pale yellow and sat in the middle of a grassy, half-acre lot that was surrounded by sunflower fields. Pretty typical for a farmhouse in North Dakota. There were a couple of clues, though, that made it clear you weren't looking at just any old farmhouse. For one thing, the site was totally enclosed in a ten-foot high fence that was topped with viciously sharp concertina wire. For another, it had a city-hall-sized flag pole and what looked like the nosecone of a missile sticking up out of the ground.

"Is that what I think it is?" I asked in awe, pointing to the nosecone.

"Probably not," Dad chuckled. "Visitors always thought that was a missile, but it's just an antenna for one of the communications systems in the launch control center."

The LCF turned out to be pretty nice inside. My favorite part was a huge recreation room with a widescreen TV and a pool table. The owner of the place, Tommy Baxter, left a note for my parents in the middle of the table. Tommy said to have a good, relaxing time and to help ourselves to canned goods and anything left in the freezer. Mom loved the size of the kitchen and the fact that it had all stainless steel appliances like you see on cooking shows. There were also three bedrooms, one with a queen-size bed and two with bunks. I planned to take the top bunk in my room even though I would have the place to myself. The top bunk just seemed cooler. To be honest, I was also thinking that if something creepy tried to get me in the middle of the night, it would probably pounce on the lower bunk first. That would at least give me time to hide or escape.

After we'd completely unloaded the van, Dad rubbed his hands together and declared, "Well, I'm going down!"

"To the launch control center?" Mandy asked expectantly. "I'm coming with you!"

"Not me," Mom said. "I once went on a tour of an LCC, and it smelled so musty. I'd rather put away groceries."

I couldn't resist seeing where my father used to be on duty for twenty-four-hour shifts. "I'll come too," I said.

Dad and Mandy and I walked through a security room which, according to Dad, used to be manned at all times by a military guard holding an M16 rifle. The security room led to what Dad called the elevator vestibule, where we found a cargo elevator—one with a metal scissor door that we could see through. We began a slow ride down to a tunnel that was seventy feet underground. The deeper we got, the more it smelled like a combination of a musty basement and saltwater.

"Yep, that's the good old *alert* smell!" Dad laughed and actually breathed more deeply. Each twenty-four-hour period in the LCC is called an alert, he explained, because officers have to keep themselves and their missiles ready for action. "Right now—at this very second—there are missileers at other bases who are on alert in active LCCs. And they rotate twenty-four hours a day, 365 days a year. People forget they're down here, but we really owe them our gratitude."

When we got off the elevator we saw two huge metal doors, similar to what you would find on bank vaults. The door on our right, which was closed, led to a room that housed support equipment for the launch control center. Dad said it was too noisy in there, so we didn't bother entering. The door on our left was chained open.

"That right there is an eight-and-a-half ton blast door!" Dad said excitedly. This was definitely a happy homecoming for him. "But the door's weight is so perfectly balanced that one guy can open or close it. Okay, now watch your heads."

We ducked down and followed Dad, waddling through a five-foot long entryway that led into the launch control center. My dad had always referred to an LCC as a capsule, and now I knew why. Picture what a pain reliever capsule looks like, a 3-D oval on its side. Now hollow out and enlarge that capsule to the size of an elementary school classroom, and imagine that it's made of super-strong steel. That's pretty much what the main structure of the control center looked like. The metal floor we were standing on was suspended from the ceiling of the capsule by enormous shock absorbers, which my dad called isolators.

"The idea with the shock isolators," Dad explained, "was that if we were attacked by nuclear weapons, the officers and equipment down here would have a better chance of survival. A lot of the force would be absorbed, and the floor would rock back and forth. See, everything here is bolted to the floor."

"This place is so cool!" Mandy exclaimed, and I had to agree with her. It would make a great hangout, much better than the crummy tree fort that Brandon and I had made in his backyard. There was a little refrigerator and toaster oven, a narrow bathroom with toilet and sink, a bed that had a thick curtain drawn around it, and even a mini-TV that got satellite reception. Best of all were the old technology gadgets that you would find in a James Bond film from the 1960s or 1970s. Several tall racks of equipment—taller than me—stood around the perimeter of the capsule and displayed circuit breakers or flashing red and yellow lights. All of the equipment was painted the same color, sea foam green, and you could hear and feel electrical power humming steadily through it all. Even the floor seemed to hum.

"Whoa! What *is* all this stuff?" I asked.

"It's mostly power and communications equipment," Dad said. "Think about it: We're seventy feet underground, isolated from the rest of the world. But the Air Force commanders had to make sure they could get messages to us whenever they needed to. And that's why we had so many different comm systems. We called them *redundant* systems. If we didn't get a message through one rack for whatever reason, we would get it through another one."

I took a seat on a comfortable airline-type chair in front of one of two consoles, each of which was the size of a church organ and had black rubber hoses cropping out of its top. These consoles had served as technology desks for crewmembers, with the commander seated at one and his deputy at the other. The phones were so old that they still had rotary dials.

"See all these lights?" Dad asked, pointing. "They're all extinguished now, but each column of lights used to represent one missile, and we would get status on the missiles by interpreting what the lights meant and what the numbers meant that came out of this little printer here."

"What about this?" Mandy asked, tapping a red metal box that was welded above the deputy's console. "It looks like a good place to hide a journal."

"Oh yeah, the all-important safe," Dad chuckled. "Visitors always wanted to look inside there, but we couldn't let them." He pointed out that the safe had two lock hasps on it. Each crewmember had his own lock, and only he knew the combination to it. If the crewmembers ever received a message telling them to get ready for war, each one would have to open his lock to get access to launch keys and Top Secret launch documents. Again, it all sounded pretty James Bondish to me, and I thought it was cool that my dad used to live in that capsule for twenty-four hours at a time, several times per month.

"And what about Bobby Swenson?" Mandy finally asked.

"And here we go," I said, shaking my head. "I knew it would come to this."

"Well, I don't know the whole story," Dad began. "But people say he was a teenager when this place was being built in 1964. I guess he came out to the site to visit his dad, one of the construction workers here, and he somehow fell into the pit they had dug."

"Poor guy," Mandy said seriously, as if she had known him or something. "And people think he's haunting this place?"

"Forget about that, sweetheart," Dad said. "I think all of us crewmembers just had overactive imaginations back then."

"But it makes sense to me," Mandy insisted. "I mean, if a person dies violently like that, some of his energy could still be moving around this place. Gretchen and I read a book that talks about how human energy can be recorded into a place, just like sound and movies can be recorded onto discs or flash drives. That's what haunting is—recorded energy that either doesn't know it can leave or chooses to hang around for some reason."

I looked at Dad and tapped my temple. "Do you want to call the psycho squad, or should I?" I asked.

"Be nice," Dad said.

I picked up the phone and put it to my ear. "What's that, Bobby, you want to go out with my sister? I don't know, you might be too *energetic* for her."

"While you're on the phone, why not give Sarah Beasley a call and ask how she likes her new boyfriend," Mandy said like a know-it-all. "She's probably going out with Brandon by now."

"Knock it off, the both of you," Dad said, losing his patience. "You know, you two need to get back on track because I'm telling you now, you're really starting to upset your mother. And then that gets me upset, and you don't want that. Understand?"

I didn't want to ruin Dad's glorious return to his old capsule. "Okay, Dad. Sorry." I made it clear that I was talking to my dad and not to Mandy.

"Me too, Daddy," Mandy said. *Daddy* again. I rolled my eyes.

"Okay then," Dad said. "Just think before you say anything to each other. If it's not something that one civilized person should say to another, then keep your mouth clamped shut. Got it?"

We both nodded "yes."

"Good," Dad continued. He took out his cell phone for some reason. "Shoot!" he said, staring at the screen. "No service."

"Kind of makes sense seventy feet underground," I teased.

"Good point," Dad laughed. "Let's see if this baby is still hooked up." He pushed two buttons on the deputy's console and we heard a dial tone through the speakerphone. "Bingo!" he said and began dialing a number.

After several rings we heard a smooth voice: "Hi, you've got Jessica at XL93. What can I do for you?"

"Hi Jessica, this is George," Dad replied kind of bashfully. "Would you please play an oldie for me? It's 'You're the Only Woman' by Ambrosia."

"We're more of a Top 40 station, George, but I should be able to find that for you."

"Great! And please dedicate it to my wife, Brenda."

Dad explained to us that he used to make song requests all the time when he was on alert, and that's why he still had the XL93 phone number in his head. Then he hurried us out of the capsule. "If we get topside in time," he said, "I'll be able to dance with your mom in the rec room."

Mandy and I both groaned. Dad led the way out of the tunnel entryway, and Mandy followed close behind. I took one more look around the place, imagining how cool it would be to have Brandon and my Cleveland Heights b-ball friends hang out there with me. That's when, out of the corner of my eye, I could swear that I saw the bed curtain flutter.

My muscles tensed and I froze in place, staring at the curtain and praying that it wouldn't move again. If something weird was present in that capsule, I didn't want to know about it. And yet I kept on staring. It's like when you're home all alone and a creaky noise slinks its way up from the basement through the heating ducts. *Was that a muffled cry? Did someone just call my name down there?* You want to know, so you put your ear close to the vent. But, then again, you don't want to know so you turn up the TV volume as a distraction. *If I don't know about it, it can't hurt me, right? Things only exist if I have evidence they exist, right?* I closed my eyes.

"Mark?"

I jumped—and I mean I *jumped*. All the tension in my muscles sprang loose at the sound of my name. It was my father, back in the capsule now and standing right behind me.

"Jeez, pal, are you okay?" he asked with concern.

"I'm fine," I said quickly and waddled through the entryway in record time.

Mandy was standing by the elevator. She looked at me kind of funny for a second and then creased her lips into that knowing half-grin of hers. She must have seen fear in my eyes.

"What's wrong with *you*?" she asked as though she had already guessed the answer.

"Nothing," I said, trying to sound normal. "Everything is just fine."

# CHAPTER FOUR

Dad's plan worked. When his dedication came on the radio, Mom squealed, "Oh George, you remembered!" And then the two of them slow danced beside the pool table. This gave Mandy time to pump me for information about what had happened in the capsule.

"What did you see?" she asked quietly.

"I didn't see anything," I said, annoyed. I didn't want to give her the satisfaction of knowing that maybe there was something to the Bobby Swenson story after all.

"Well, you sure looked pretty pale for a kid who didn't see anything."

"It smelled down there, in case you didn't notice," I said. "You looked pale too."

"Okay, let's go down and try again," she suggested.

"Just forget about it."

"You're afraid to go down there with me, aren't you? See, I knew it."

That was too much for me to take. "Yeah, right. I'd just rather go back down by myself, that's all." As soon as those words left my lips, I knew I would wind up regretting them.

"Prove it," Mandy taunted. "I'll bet you ten dollars you couldn't stay alone in the capsule—all the way in—for a half-hour."

"You're on!" I said. My pride was at stake. Leave it to a twin to bring out major stupidity in you.

25

*******

Standing in the tunnel again with the enormous blast door chained open before me, I decided to make a quick entry into the capsule. If I thought about it too much, I would chicken out for sure. I clutched my chess set and book, lowered my shoulder, and charged into the entryway like a football player crashing through the team banner before the big game. I was thrilled to find no ghost waiting for me on the other side.

I still didn't feel at ease, though, and now I was really wishing my friends from Cleveland Heights could be with me. I knew it would be a long half-hour if I didn't confront my fear right off the bat, so the first thing I did was march right over to the bed. I yanked the curtain all the way open and discovered . . . nothing at all! That was a relief. I told myself that it must have been a breeze that moved the curtain, but then I immediately doubted this explanation. Sure, the capsule had a ventilation system to provide fresh air to the place, but the curtain was way too heavy to be pushed around by a puff of air. So I decided that I hadn't seen anything at all; that my mind had played a trick on me. And that was that. Mandy was wrong about all the haunting nonsense, and I would be thrilled to share that bit of news with her.

I turned on the TV to keep me company. Some nature show came on and I plunked myself down in the comfy chair at the commander's console. I set up my chess board on a little table next to a rack of communications equipment.

"Survivable Low Frequency Communications System," I read aloud from the metal nameplate on the rack. "Boy, there's a mouthful for you."

Hearing my own voice helped to calm my nerves, and I appreciated finding the word "Survivable" in the rack's name; I took that as a sign that I would get out of the capsule alive. I opened my book to reenact another Bobby Fischer-Boris Spassky match. I looked at my watch and figured that the thirty minutes would go by in a hurry while playing chess. Hey, maybe I would settle in for a full hour if I felt like it.

About ten minutes into the match I was completely focused and relaxed. Spassky had just made a move that would allow Fischer to bring down a rook and confine Spassky's king to the back rank. Spassky must not have seen this.

"Your move, Bobby," I said aloud in my best Russian accent.

As I reached for Fischer's rook, it— It started to move on its own! The rook slid down the board to the exact position indicated in my book. I suddenly felt dizzy and hot. I thought I might pass out. *Please don't move again*, I pleaded silently with the rook. My brain was buzzing with the capsule's electrical hum and my insides were on fire. When I was sick at home one day, I accidentally took a mouthful of steaming-hot honey tea and then stupidly swallowed it instead of spitting it out. It burned all the way down and pooled like lava in my stomach. That same pain was tearing me up again.

I was as still as a stone, focused completely on the board and trying to smooth out my rapid breathing. *Please don't move again.* There was no way I imagined what I had just seen, and I knew that no breeze on Earth—or even under it—could slide a chess piece like that. *Please do <u>not</u> move again.* I closed my eyes and listened to the host of the TV show babbling on about the migration of geese, but it was like I was suddenly underwater and his garbled words were barely reaching my ears from the surface. I opened my eyes again and stared at the board. *Just stay still now.*

The electrical hum of the capsule crept up through my feet and made my knees vibrate. I rehashed in my mind how Mandy defined a haunting, as the recorded energy of someone who died a violent death. *Am I feeling some of that energy now? Is this why knees shake—like mine are shaking now—when people are scared?*

And then Spassky's bishop moved to a new square—again, just as written in my book. Whatever energy was in the capsule, it knew how to read and it was getting impatient with me for just sitting there. Now one of Fischer's pawns started to move, and before I knew it I was in the tunnel junction outside the capsule, scrambling up the ladder that was bolted to the wall beside the elevator shaft. There was no way I was going to waste time on that slow elevator.

"Oh man! Oh man!" I was saying on my way up. I tried to shout the words, but they came out just above a whisper.

When I reached the top of the ladder I saw a hand extended over the edge, and I screamed like a first-grade girl. Mandy leaned over the ladder and said, "Come on, it's me." I had never been so happy to see my twin as at that moment. I took her hand and climbed out of the shaft.

"He's down there, isn't he?" Mandy asked with a satisfied smile. Her eyes were wide with excitement.

"Something . . . is," I wheezed, out of breath from my climb.

"Oh, it's Bobby," Mandy said with authority. "This is so freaky and amazing! We've got to go back down and help him." She pushed the button to call the elevator back up.

"No . . . way!" I said, starting to catch my breath.

"I'll go myself if you won't come with me."

"Then I'll tell Mom and Dad," I warned. It sounded lame—like something Mandy would say to me—but I had to protect her. Who knew what this thing was capable of doing? She tried to convince me that it would be a cool adventure and that everything would work out okay. I wouldn't budge, though.

"After I do a little research on this in town," Mandy said, "then you'll come around."

"Don't count on it," I warned. We left the elevator vestibule and walked through the security room.

"You owe me ten dollars, by the way," she said. "Or ten-eighty, if you're feeling generous."

"Shut up."

"That would be, like, Ten-Point-Eight dollars in case you're wondering," Mandy added with a cold laugh. She walked briskly into the recreation room, where our parents were watching the same nature show that had been on in the capsule.

*******

Last fall, Brandon and I had been shooting hoops after school one day when three older boys starting messing with us. We didn't recognize them from the neighborhood, but they had to be at least a year older than us. The tallest of the three sprinted up and grabbed the rebound from one of Brandon's shots before I had a chance. When the boy wouldn't give the ball back, Brandon called him and his friends a pretty bad name.

"So that's how you wanna play this?" the tall boy said with a huge, satisfied smile. He set the ball down and put a foot on it like it was the head of a grizzly bear he had just shot dead. "Come and get it, little boy."

"Let's just go," I said nervously to Brandon, and all three of the older boys started cracking up.

"You better listen to your little friend there," one of the boys taunted Brandon, who just stared at the ball and said nothing.

"Come on," I said quietly. My heart was thumping in my throat. I had a reputation at school for a sarcastic sense of humor and an aggressive style on the basketball court. I wanted people to think I was a pretty tough guy, but the truth was I had never been in a real fight before. And I didn't want to start now—especially when Brandon and I were outnumbered by older guys.

Without warning, Brandon suddenly charged the tall boy and kicked the ball out from under his foot. The chase was on. Brandon and I took off after the ball, which had sailed beyond the blacktop and was now rolling down the sidewalk. The three older boys ran after us. *Oh man, oh man!* jolted through my mind. *Don't fall! Don't fall!*

Fear gripped me, buzzing through my spine and legs in an electric rush. I felt imaginary fists and feet striking me all over my body. My eyes were stinging, and I'm ashamed to say that a few tears streaked down my face as I ran.

Brandon and I are both fast runners, but once he scooped up the ball, that slowed him down and I got pretty far ahead. Reggie Williams, one of our classmates, just happened to look out his front window as we shot past his house. "The way that boy was running," Reggie likes to say, meaning me, "I swear he could have beat my brother in the dash by a tenth of a second, easy!" And that's where the Ten-Point-Eight nickname came from: Reggie's brother holds the local high school record—10.9 seconds—for the 100-meter dash. Reggie told everybody this stupid story, over and over again. "Mark ran so fast that day that it brought tears to his eyes!" he would add, and of course his little audience would laugh.

Throughout the rest of the school year, some kids still referred to me as Ten-Point-Eight from time to time. I pretended that it didn't bother me, but it did. Brandon knew I didn't like the name, so at least he never called me that. That would have really hurt, hearing it from him.

# CHAPTER FIVE

Mandy and I sat at the Foxtrot-Zero picnic table the day after I'd seen the chess pieces move on their own. Morning rain pelted the huge umbrella overhead, and every now and then a gust of wind made the pole squeal as the umbrella strained to free itself. The air felt so sticky.

We agreed that it was best to keep our parents in the dark about the situation in the capsule. Why worry them? Between Dad's writing and Mom's going to classes, they both had important reasons to stay put in North Dakota for a month. And if we scared Mom into moving, we knew that our family couldn't afford to live in a Grand Forks hotel for so many nights.

"It's not like we're in danger here," Mandy said. "Bobby didn't strangle you or anything, even when he had you all alone down there."

I shuddered at the memory of being alone with Bobby, or whatever energy it was. "Maybe I got out just in time, though. You never know. If anything bizarre starts happening topside, then we'll tell Mom and Dad for sure."

"Nothing will happen up here," Mandy said confidently. "I mean, I'm sure Bobby could go anywhere if he wanted to. He either doesn't know he can, or he has a good reason for staying where he is."

"Yeah, yeah. I've already heard your haunting theory."

"It's not just mine. I read it in a book."

"Whatever. Just promise me you'll stay away from the capsule. Better yet, promise you won't even go in the security room because once you're in there, I know you wouldn't be able to resist getting on the elevator."

"I'll promise for now," Mandy reluctantly agreed. "As long as you promise to listen with an open mind after I do some research on Bobby in town. I can't find anything about his death on the Internet."

I sighed and made a thumbs-up. She did the same, and we pressed our thumbs to the middle of each other's forehead. We've been doing that to seal promises for as long as I can remember. I'm not even sure anymore which one of us made it up.

"And if it turns out that it's Bobby haunting the capsule, we'll have to help him," Mandy said firmly. Thunder rang out in the distance and rolled lazily for several seconds. The umbrella pole squealed in response.

"What would we need to get involved for?" I asked. "We never even knew the kid."

"Remember the time we found that two-year-old locked inside a car at the mall?" Mandy asked.

"Of course. What about it?" I got upset recalling the image of that little boy crying his lungs out in his car seat.

"We didn't know the baby, but we got involved anyway."

"That was different. That may have been a life-or-death situation."

"This may be too. Plus, if someone needs help, you help if you can. It's the right thing to do."

I didn't have an argument for that. I thought about Mandy leaning in toward the car and saying, "It's gonna be okay, baby," while I flagged down a mall security officer. When the mother eventually got back to the car, she said she didn't see what the big deal was: She had been gone only fifteen minutes and the car windows were cracked.

She was actually mad at Mandy and me for "butting in" to her business. I felt like saying, "It's more than just your windows that are cracked, lady," but Mandy and I were too shocked to say anything.

"Pretend like Bobby is Brandon, and this is your second chance," Mandy said now, under the table umbrella. "I know that if you could relive that day, you would do something to help him."

Mandy's words made me furious because I *did* relive that day over and over again, at least in my mind. And since when did my sister become a professional guidance counselor, thinking it was her place to give me advice?

"I . . . did . . . *not* . . . hear . . . Brandon . . . call . . . for . . . help," I said, leaning in and bouncing my words off her face one at a time. "I . . . did . . . *not* . . . know . . . he . . . fell."

I stood up, smacked the fringe of the umbrella, and began walking toward the house in the rain. Lightning flashed into existence and released fingers of energy to probe the sky over nearby sunflower fields.

"Mark, I'm sorry," Mandy called out over the rippling thunder, but I wouldn't look back. "I didn't mean—"

I entered the house and slammed the door behind me.

*******

The next few days at Foxtrot-Zero were dry, but uneventful and boring. Mom left for the university at nine o'clock each morning, and we didn't see her again until about three in the afternoon. Dad sat in their bedroom during those same hours and clicked the keys on his laptop, working on his book. Mandy and I tried to get Dad to discuss his story, but he had this weird idea that talking about it could sap his creative energy. "It takes place in Cleveland and it involves a corrupt politician," was all he would say. *Great,* I thought. *You drag us from Cleveland Heights to North Dakota so you can write a story about our hometown.*

I shot baskets for hours every day, and even that became boring since I had no one to challenge. When Mandy wasn't reading books or writing in her journal, she did at least play pool with me. We agreed to a truce because we had no one else to hang out with. Mandy was being extra nice to me, actually, because she wanted me to go into town with her. She had asked to go with our mother, but Mom said both of us would have to go because she didn't want Mandy spending the whole day in a new town completely on her own. I refused. I wasn't looking to make any new friends now; I just wanted to get back to my old ones in Ohio.

But after three days, total mind-numbing boredom set in. I realized how bored I had become when I finished mowing the lawn and just stared at the sunflower fields surrounding the LCF. It was cool to see how the flower heads turned to follow the sun throughout the day; it was like they were looking up into the eyes of some mighty hypnotist. I could swear that the plants had already grown several inches during the short time we had been there. I got this idea to adopt one plant and measure its current height, and then check it every day to record its growth. I even considered setting up a camera to do a time-lapse series of my sunflower turning its head throughout the course of one day. And that's when it hit me: "Dude, you need a life," I said aloud.

So, the next morning Mandy and I joined our mother in the van for the forty-minute ride to the university, UND. I thought that was a crazy amount of time to spend driving each day—eighty minutes roundtrip—but Mom said it was easy to get used to.

Mom drove once around the campus before parking, pointing out our perimeter for the day. "Stay within this area, and *stay together*," she warned. Mandy and I had heard the "stay together" command since we were toddlers, and I'm not sure Mom realized how old we were getting. I noticed a park just across from campus, and I asked if we could go there as well because I saw some kids in the middle of a basketball game. "Okay," Mom agreed. "But no farther than that." Mom showed us where to meet her for lunch on a grassy field, which she called a quadrangle, right behind the Chester Fritz Library. She kissed both of us on the cheek before heading into her classroom building. It was kind of weird dropping our mom off to school instead of the other way around.

"Chester Fritz, here we come!" Mandy said happily.

"No way, Mandy," I said. "I didn't drive forty minutes just to sit in a library all day. No way."

"I'll make you a deal," she began. "Give me just one hour in there, and then you get to pick where we go for the rest of the day."

I threw my hands up. "Fine," I said and followed her inside. When you give up in a chess match it's called *conceding*. I've learned over the years that it's best to concede to Mandy in the game of life when she really has her mind set on something. It's usually not worth an argument.

Mandy marched up to the desk of a silver-haired reference librarian, and within two minutes it was like they were old friends. When the lady stood up to shake Mandy's hand, I was surprised by how short she was: maybe four-ten. Mrs. Langley, as her nametag read, said she had a granddaughter about our age, and she thought it was wonderful that we were doing a research project during summer vacation.

"It's either this or watch sunflowers grow," I said sarcastically.

"I see," Mrs. Langley said, looking not one bit amused.

"Did you grow up with a smart-aleck brother too?" Mandy asked.

"Actually, yes I did," Mrs. Langley said, raising her eyebrows. "Two of them." The girls shared a good laugh at my expense.

Mandy shot me the evil eye and then politely asked her new little friend to see local newspapers from 1964. Dad had told us that Foxtrot-Zero was built that year, so I knew Mandy was trying to track down information on Bobby Swenson, or whatever that strange force was that still had control of my chess board and book. Who knows how many games had been reenacted in the capsule? Maybe my pieces were moving around the board right at that moment. I shuddered at the thought.

Mrs. Langley explained that old newspaper stories were available only on what she called "feesh." I felt like asking, "Feesh? What happens if they sweem away?" But I bit my tongue; I was outnumbered two to one. She led us to a metal cabinet where a sign read "Microfiche." *Oh, so that's how you spell it*, I thought.

Mrs. Langley explained that microfiche—or just "fiche" for short—is like a mini overhead transparency that has pages printed on it in microscopic form. A special machine illuminates the fiche and magnifies the text so you can read it or even print it out. Mrs. Langley handed Mandy an envelope that contained every issue of *The Grand Forks Herald* for 1964. Before she had a chance to demonstrate how to use the reader machine, though, she got called away by another librarian.

I laughed when Mandy spent the next minute searching unsuccessfully for the On switch. Any stranger passing by would have thought Mandy was a blind girl trying to get a mental image of the machine. One stranger—a boy our age wearing glasses with small rectangular lenses—finally came over and offered assistance.

"Here you go," the kid said shyly and flipped a switch under the machine. He was what my parents would call a towhead because of his extremely blond hair. And he had pale skin to match, like he never spent time in the sun. The humongously thick book he was holding offered a clue as to what he did with his time.

"Oh, thank you so much!" Mandy cooed. She sounded impressed, like this guy was a genius for knowing where a switch was.

"I can show you how to use this if you'd like," he said awkwardly and set down his book. Mandy read the title aloud, *Piercing the Veil: True Accounts of the Paranormal.*

"Wow!" she exclaimed. "What a cool book that must be!"

"You could borrow it when I'm done," the boy said with more confidence now. "If you want to."

*My sister has met her soul mate in the Chester Fritz Library*, I was thinking. *Yes!*

The kid, who introduced himself as Alex, slid a fiche between two pieces of glass and demonstrated how to advance from one page of the newspaper to the next. That's when I decided to head outside to the basketball court. I knew our mom wanted Mandy and me to stick together, but I wasn't about to waste my summer vacation watching two kids play a game of "Go Feesh." I told Mandy I would meet her on the quadrangle ten minutes before our lunch with Mom.

"Hey, Mom wants—" Mandy began.

"See ya," I said.

I got to the park a little too late. There was only one player left on the basketball court, a tall girl with dark brown hair pulled back in a ponytail. She was at the free-throw line draining one shot after another, and most of them were swishes. She looked so focused that I didn't think she had even noticed me. Suddenly, she rested the ball against her hip and said, "You just move in?"

"Only for a month," I said. "House-sitting," I added automatically and regretted saying it; it sounded lame.

"In it or on it?" she asked seriously. I must have looked confused. "The house I mean," she said with a chuckle. "It was a stupid joke. I'm Aggie. Aggie Burke." She walked over to me and shook my hand firmly. She had sparkly brown eyes, a few freckles sprinkled across her nose, and a great tan. She looked to be about my age, eleven, but she was also a whole head taller than me.

"I'm Mark Cousineau," I said looking up at her. I felt like I was talking to a sports statue that had just come to life. She used the back of her arm to wipe sweat off her forehead.

"Take a few warm-up shots and we'll go best of ten from the line," she announced. She walked over to the fence and drank from a water bottle while I got loose. I have to be honest: I was nervous. I wanted to make a good first impression, and the possibility of being beaten by a girl just wasn't too thrilling. If the guys back home ever found out, they would dog me for a week straight.

Aggie insisted that I go first, and I made seven out of ten free-throws. Very respectable, especially when you consider that some NBA pros shoot below seventy percent from the line. And then it was Aggie's turn. After sinking eight in a row she said, "Hey, nice game." She wasn't being sarcastic, and I could tell that winning wasn't everything to her; she just loved being out there on the court the way an artist loves being in a studio. "You mind if I shoot the last two?" she asked good-naturedly.

"Go for it," I said and actually wanted her to make both. That's exactly what she did, and I lunged over to give her a high-five.

"Cool!" she said with a bright smile. I'm not sure if she meant cool that she had nailed all ten shots, or cool that I high-fived her. Either way, it really didn't matter.

We went on to play two games of one-on-one. I lost both, but I came close in the second one. Nobody loves to lose, but I had to admit that she was a better, taller player than I was. She had great dribbling skills and was just as comfortable driving to the left side of the basket as the right.

"Wow!" I said and shook my head as we walked off the court. "When you're eventually playing in the WNBA, I'll say I used to go one-on-one with you back in the day."

Aggie just laughed.

"And that I used to kick your butt," I added, wiping sweat from my eyes.

"Yeah, dream on!" Aggie said and gave me a playful push. "Here, I haven't opened this one yet." She tossed me a bottled water.

"Thanks, I definitely could use it."

Aggie checked her watch and said she had to leave. "But I'm here every day. Usually with some other guys too. Come and play whenever you feel like it."

"Okay, thanks again," I said, raising my bottle to her. "Bye."

"Bye."

We both started walking in the same direction. "Well, maybe *not* bye!" Aggie laughed. As it turned out, she lived on campus in one of the dormitories, which I thought was pretty cool. She said her mom was the superintendent for

Squires Hall, making sure everything was okay for the students who lived there. I felt like moving in myself when Aggie explained that Squires was an all-female dorm. Imagine—a whole dorm full of nothing but college girls! I could be their mascot or something.

"Do you have any brothers or sisters?" I asked as we approached the library.

"Just one brother," she said. She rolled her eyes and pointed toward the door. "Right there."

Unreal! Alex was walking down the library steps with Mandy. We all met up on the fringe of the grass and were shocked to discover that we were two sets of twins born only three months apart; Alex and Aggie were older than us. I swear, twins never looked more different than those two. Aggie was a bronze statue towering over a pasty-white lawn gnome.

"This is incredible!" Mandy exclaimed. "What are the odds of twins finding each other without knowing that their own twin was meeting the other twin? That sounds confusing, but you all know what I mean."

"Speak for yourself," I said.

"Shut up!" Mandy was the one to say that for a change.

"I'm glad to see we're not the only twins who don't get along all the time," Aggie said.

"Yeah, be careful around my sister," Alex warned and pushed up his glasses. "She probably didn't tell you, but Aggie is short for *Agony*."

Instead of saying "shut up," Aggie punched Alex in the arm, a good hard slug that left him rubbing his shoulder. "It's Agatha," she said to Mandy and me. Agatha or Agony—I didn't care which. I thought this girl was all right.

"See you tomorrow," the twins said and started climbing the Chester Fritz steps.

I was confused. "Hey, do you live in a dorm or a library?" I asked.

"Check this out," Aggie said. She pointed at a dormitory building across the street, about a hundred yards away. "That's Squires Hall right there. Keep your eyes on that door."

Aggie and Alex entered the library, but within two minutes they appeared at the Squires door. They gave us a big wave and I threw my hands in the air, as if to say, "How did you do that?"

"Tunnels!" they called out through megaphones formed with their hands.

*******

At the dinner table that evening, Mom said that if I had ever lived through a North Dakota winter, I wouldn't be asking why UND's buildings are connected by tunnels. "It gets brutally cold out there," she said. "We're talking daytime highs that are below zero, and nighttime lows that are way, way below zero."

You'd never know it from the hot, muggy air that hit me as I walked out to the basketball hoop after eating. Mandy followed and actually tossed the ball back to me after each shot while I played around-the-world. I knew she wanted something.

"So, did you find what you were looking for in the old newspapers?" I asked.

"Not yet," Mandy replied. She caught the basketball off a bounce and held it against her belly with both hands. She didn't look nearly as comfortable with the ball as Aggie had looked in town. "Come on, don't you think it was weird meeting another set of twins like that?"

"Weird coincidence," I allowed. "Now gimme the ball."

"Maybe more than just a coincidence," she persisted, holding her ground—and the ball. "It's like it was meant to happen."

"What's that supposed to mean?"

"It's like a team is coming together. Maybe they're supposed to help us with the Bobby Swenson . . . situation."

I just stared at my sister for a while. "Did you already say something to Alex about that?"

"No. I told him I was looking through the papers for a report on how Grand Forks has changed over the past fifty years."

"Good," I said, relieved. "Don't say anything about Bobby Swenson. Alex and Aggie are gonna think we're insane—or at least you."

"We'll see," she said unconvincingly. She bounce-passed the ball to me, finally, and headed for the house.

"Promise you won't say anything," I called out. I made the thumbs-up sign and started after her, but she wouldn't even look back.

"We'll see," she repeated and went inside.

# CHAPTER SIX

The next day on the basketball court was great. Aggie and I teamed up to take on two older guys in a long, physical game. Thanks to Aggie, who scored more than half of our points, we won twenty-one baskets to seventeen. We sauntered off the court drenched in sweat and feeling like we owned the place. After we finished our water and swished the empty bottles into a recycling can, Aggie took off running toward campus, yelling, "It's a race!"

"Cheater!" I shouted with a laugh and took off after her. I caught up pretty easily, and by the time we reached the quadrangle I was at least twenty yards ahead.

"Whew! Your brother is fast!" Aggie exclaimed when we reached Mandy and Alex.

I stared at my sister. *Oh, don't bring up the whole Ten-Point-Eight business,* my eyes were pleading. Mandy just nodded her head and said, matter-of-factly, "One of the fastest back home." *Thank you, Sister.*

"You're not gonna believe this!" Alex exclaimed, waving papers at Aggie and me. "We printed out three newspaper stories about Bobby Swenson from November and December, 1964."

*Oh boy, here we go,* I was thinking.

"Bobby *who*?" Aggie asked.

"You'll find out," Alex said excitedly. "Just be patient for a while."

We sat in the shade of a tall oak tree while Mandy gave a summary of the first article. In November 1964, sixteen-year-old Bobby drove out to the Foxtrot-Zero construction site to see his father, the foreman. Mr. Swenson had forgotten his lunch box at home, so Bobby brought it to him. Just as workers began pouring concrete into the seventy-foot hole, Bobby slipped in and was killed instantly. By the time a frantic Mr. Swenson was lowered into the pit, only his son's back was visible; the rest was covered in mucky concrete.

"Isn't that grisly?" Alex asked.

"Gross!" Aggie responded.

I didn't say anything, but thinking about the way Bobby died made me feel a little queasy. There's an elevator ride at Cedar Point called Demon Drop where you get to experience a free-fall for three seconds. I force myself to go on that ride every summer because I don't want my friends to think I'm chicken. That feeling of my stomach up in my throat is terrifying to me, though, and I pitied Bobby for having that sensation as his last one on Earth. He must have known on the way down that his life was about to be snuffed out. I cringed.

"I still don't get why you two are so concerned about something that happened fifty years ago," Aggie observed.

"Foxtrot-Zero is the place where Mark and I are staying," Mandy explained.

"Okay," I said and tried to rescue the situation before it got totally out of hand. "So someone got killed there a long time ago. It's really not a big deal anymore."

"If you ask me, a haunted launch control center really *is* a big deal," Alex pounced, sounding like a lawyer in the courtroom.

"Haunted?" Aggie echoed. "What makes you say it's haunted?"

"Weren't you listening to what Mandy just told you?" Alex replied, exasperated. "Jeez, how could it *not* be haunted after something like that?"

"Plus, Mark has seen weird things down there," Mandy added. "Twice already."

Aggie looked to me for an explanation. Her sparkly brown eyes were open wide; she was definitely intrigued. I tried to sound as casual as possible while I told her about the flapping curtain and the moving chess pieces. "But maybe my mind just tricked me into seeing things," I added.

"This all sounds crazy," Aggie responded with a dazed look.

"See?" I said smartly to Mandy and Alex. "She agrees with me."

"Crazy *cool* I mean!" Aggie added with a mischievous grin. "I'd love to check it out for myself."

"We were hoping you'd say that!" Mandy exclaimed, and both she and Alex gave Aggie a friendly slap on the shoulder.

"Yeah!" Alex said excitedly. "We're gonna see if we can release this kid. Mandy and I hope we can help him find his way to . . . you know, the other side."

"Whoa, keep your voice down," I warned and looked around the quadrangle. All clear; no one was close enough to overhear our conversation. "Okay, now this is really getting out of control," I continued. "Forget about it. If you two want to go around acting like nut cases, then go right ahead. Just leave Aggie and me out of this." Aggie had that grin on her face again. "Right, Aggie?" I asked weakly.

"I don't know," she responded and tapped the printouts that Alex was holding. "Let's hear more."

The second newspaper article was a long one that described Bobby's closed-casket wake and funeral. Alex read aloud: "The entire junior class from Red River High School attended the ceremony to bid farewell to their young classmate. Joseph Blanchard delivered a tearful eulogy describing his friend as well-rounded, well-liked, and full of leadership potential."

"You recognize that name, don't you?" Mandy interrupted. "Joe Blanchard is the guy running for the U.S. Senate."

I remembered seeing billboards and TV ads for Blanchard's campaign. His slogan was, "It's time to unite and move forward," which I didn't think was too original; every candidate says pretty much the same thing.

The 1964 newspaper article went on to explain that the District Attorney's office was considering charges against Mr. Swenson for child endangerment. The charge was that as the site foreman, Mr. Swenson should have ensured his son remained a safe distance from the pit.

"Now here's where it gets really interesting," Alex mused. He read aloud again: "A complicating factor is a fifty-thousand-dollar life insurance policy that the Swensons had taken out on Bobby just one month earlier. According to Mrs. Swenson, the policy had been purchased as an investment for her son."

"See, the plot thickens," Mandy offered, which is an expression that she and Gretchen use back home to describe a twist in one of their mysteries. "Maybe the dad *pushed* him."

These words brought back the Demon Drop queasiness for me. Could there really exist in the whole world a man so evil that he would push his son to his death, just to collect an insurance payout?

The third newspaper article, from a month later, stated that the District Attorney decided not to press charges after all. Mandy read the DA's words: "We have discovered no evidence that Mr. Swenson intentionally contributed to the death of his son. And although we might make a case for negligence, I would suggest that the Swenson family is suffering enough already, especially now that the Christmas season has arrived."

"And that's all we could find about the case," Alex said with disappointment. "There's nothing else in the newspapers from that year or the next."

"Well, then that means the story's over," I concluded.

"Not as far as *I'm* concerned," Alex objected. "Maybe this kid was killed by his own father. We need to find out."

"Murder, she wrote!" Mandy added dramatically,

This was a reference to a lame old TV show that Mandy watches on DVD with our Grandma Cousineau whenever we sleep over there. *Murder, She Wrote!* features some lady named Jessica who solves murder mystery after murder mystery in her tiny town of Cabot Cove, Maine. "Cabot Cove has got to be the most dangerous town in the whole world," Grandpa always teases, adding, "Jessica would be better off living in the middle of a war zone, for crying out loud!" He and I laugh, and Grandma and Mandy shush us. That's our routine.

"We'll get these two to sleep over at Foxtrot-Zero sometime soon," Mandy decided, nodding at Alex and Aggie. "They'll help us solve the mystery."

"No way!" I protested. "There's absolutely no way I'm getting involved in this." I didn't admit it, of course, but I was afraid just thinking about going down in the capsule again.

*******

Two nights later the four of us were seated in the Foxtrot-Zero capsule, arranged in a tight circle with our knees touching. Mandy and Alex were acting like experts on supernatural phenomena, and it was their idea that we had to touch "to allow for a continual flow of energy." *Yeah, whatever.* The overhead lights were dimmed, oozing an eerie glow onto the faces of my fellow twins.

A song called "Come a Little Bit Closer" was playing quietly in the background on Mandy's boombox. Mandy and Alex had found an old *Billboard Magazine* at the library that listed the top five songs for the week that Bobby died in 1964, and then they burned those songs onto a CD. Their idea was that familiar music would make Bobby more likely to visit us. Here's what Mandy had written on the CD case insert:

- *Leader of the Pack* – Shangri-Las
- *Baby Love* – Supremes
- *Come a Little Bit Closer* – Jay and the Americans
- *She's Not There* – Zombies
- *Ringo* – Lorne Greene

There we were, trying to make contact with a dead guy, and the next song to play was by a group called the Zombies. I didn't like the sound of that. And as far as the Jay and the Americans song was concerned, I would have preferred "Stay Far Away."

Let me back up and explain how we all came to be together that night in the capsule. Arranging the sleepover was awkward because we pretended that Alex was my friend and Aggie was Mandy's. My parents are pretty cool, but they would have been concerned if I had said something like, "Can my friend Aggie, who happens to be a girl, please sleep over?" So, as far as my parents were concerned, Alex was my new best buddy. Some buddy; he had brought a chess set in his backpack and beaten me two games out of three. *One Burke twin beats me in basketball and the other one beats me in chess,* I was thinking. *Terrific.*

Speaking of chess, when the four of us had sneaked down to the capsule around midnight, I found that my board had been reset for a fresh game. "Whoa!" I whispered.

Back to the circle . . . Mandy placed a tall white candle in the middle of us and lit it. For several seconds—it felt like minutes—we all just sat there staring at the flickering flame. The soft music and steady electrical hum of old technology seemed to me like the quiet before a storm.

"Okay, is that it?" I finally asked, ready to snatch up my chess set and head for the elevator.

"You want me to start?" Alex asked Mandy.

"Sure, go ahead."

"Dear Bobby," Alex began awkwardly.

I looked at Aggie and we both started cracking up. It was the kind of laugh that starts as a snort and then jumps to your lips.

"What, are you writing the kid a letter or something?" Aggie said.

"Gimme a break," Alex said, offended. "It's not like I've actually done this before."

"Let's have everybody close their eyes and get serious," Mandy suggested.

I didn't want to be a total spoilsport, so I did as I was told. "Start again," Mandy whispered. With my eyes closed I became more aware of the electrical vibrations going through the floor to the racks of equipment. The energy zinged up to my knees. It also shimmied up my spine and split off east and west when it reached my neck. Both of my shoulder blades were twitching, but I did my best to keep my knees still so the others wouldn't know how creeped out I was.

"Bobby?" Alex said. I flinched at the sound of Bobby's name slicing through the silence. I couldn't help it.

"The four of us are here tonight," Alex continued, "because we believe *you're* here too, and we want to see if you need some kind of help."

"We don't want you to be all alone anymore," Mandy added. "You have the power to move on to something better if you want to. I don't know if time still means anything to you, but you passed away fifty years ago."

"You fell into the pit where your father was working," Alex said. "Now, if there's something holding you back here in this launch control center—anything we can help you with—then please give us a sign."

The electrical hum became more than I could bear, and I opened my eyes. The others soon opened theirs as well, just in time to see the candle flicker crazily in every direction and then blow out.

"What the heck!" I yelled and jumped to my feet. "Let's go!" I demanded. I must have had a crazed look in my eyes because everyone just sat there and stared at me.

And then we heard a *ka-chunk, ka-chunk* sound from around the corner, on the other side of the commander's console. We rushed over to find that the communications system with the long name had come back to life and was slowly printing a message. This was incredible because my father had told me that, other than the telephones, none of the comm equipment had worked since the Air Force shut down Foxtrot-Zero in 1998! Yet there it was, *ka-chunking* away while a narrow strip of paper scrolled out of a slot in the middle of the rack. The paper looked like the receipt that comes out of a grocery store cash register. "This shouldn't be happening," I mumbled.

Just below the slot was a little glass window that was illuminated while the message printed. Mandy kneeled down and stared into the window. I couldn't believe she was doing this. Part of me—a big part of me—wanted to run out the door, but something kept me riveted there in front of the rack. *This can't be happening.*

"What does it say?" Alex asked excitedly.

"So far, PAPA UNIFORM SIERRA," Mandy reported.

"Oh man!" Alex said. "This has something to do with his father! The first word is Papa."

"And maybe his dad was in the military before he became a construction worker," Aggie added. "Maybe that's why the second word is Uniform."

"Hold on!" I suddenly cried out, and everyone looked at me. I had a theory of my own to contribute, and the thought of it gave me the courage to speak. "He might just be spelling something out. Like A is Alpha, B is Bravo, C is Charlie. They use that junk in the military. That's why this place is called Foxtrot; it was the sixth site that the Air Force opened here, just like the letter F is the sixth letter of the alphabet." My father had explained all this to me before we even came to North Dakota.

As Mandy turned to look through the window again, the *ka-chunking* stopped and the little light went out. Alex figured out that pressing a button next to the window made the paper advance quickly through the slot. After the entire message appeared beyond the slot, Mandy ripped it off. She stood up and read the message aloud:

PAPA UNIFORM SIERRA

HOTEL ECHO DELTA

"That's P-U-S-H-E-D," I said.

"Pushed!" everyone yelled together.

"So somebody *did* kill Bobby!" Alex exclaimed.

Mandy kneeled in front of the communications rack again and looked into the little window. "Is that true, Bobby? Give us another message."

Just then, Telephone Button #1 started flashing on both the commander's and deputy's consoles, accompanied by a *bip-bip* sound. "Oh man, he's calling us!" I said in disbelief. Mandy dashed over to the commander's console and pressed the two buttons that our father had pressed when he called the radio station. "Um, hello?" she said with her head cocked to one side. My ears felt hot in anticipation of a ghost's voice. Would it be a hoarse whisper? Would we understand what Bobby had to say? Would he be hacked off at us for disturbing his rest?

"This . . . is . . . your . . . father," we heard over the speakerphone. It was Dad all right, and I knew he was talking through his teeth. *Busted!* Dad went on to say that he and Mom had searched for us outside and that neither one of them was too happy about that. "Come . . . up . . . now!" he ordered.

"Well, you all heard the man," I said and picked up my chess set and book before heading toward the blast door.

In the kitchenette, Mandy turned off the CD. "Hey, I can't get this out," she said while yanking on the boombox plug. I tried also—until my fingers hurt—but with no luck. I actually felt a little shock.

"Maybe Bobby wants it down here," Aggie said seriously. "Just leave it."

Sure enough, as we were getting on the elevator we heard "Leader of the Pack" begin to play. We all looked at each other with wide eyes and laughed nervously. Mandy put out her hand, palm-side down, and the rest of us stacked our hands on top of hers like athletes do at the beginning of a game. Well, *our* game had just begun, that's for sure.

On the slow elevator ride up, my mind raced—not with thoughts about what my upset parents had planned for us, but rather with thoughts about Bobby. Did his father push him to his death just to get the insurance money? Did his mother play a part in the scheme? Why did Bobby choose that *ka-chunking* rack to communicate through, and what else would he be able to tell us? There were so many unanswered questions. I looked at my fellow twins, feeling nervous and excited to be part of their team.

# CHAPTER SEVEN

We decided to work in two mini-teams to make the most efficient use of our time. Mandy and Alex would begin by snooping around Red River High School. Alex had read that it's a good idea to have a picture of a deceased person in the room that his energy haunts; you increase the odds that the energy will take human form and communicate more freely. That was a scary thought, I have to admit.

"Why would having a picture matter?" I asked.

"Think about it," Alex said. "If you had to draw yourself from memory right now, how accurate would the picture be? Close your eyes for a second and try to picture yourself as clearly as possible."

I closed my eyes and was surprised at how difficult it was for me to create a mental image of myself, even though I see that face in the mirror every day of my life. I told Alex that I couldn't do it very well.

"Plus," Mandy added, "think about how much more difficult it would be to base your image on a fifty-year-old memory. We're hoping that when Bobby sees a picture of himself when he was sixteen, that'll spark something."

The first assignment for Aggie and me was to find out if Bobby's parents were still living and, if so, where they were. We knew from the newspaper articles that the father's name was Robert J. Swenson and the mother's was Frances L. Swenson. The Internet and the local phonebook showed no sign of them, so we went to visit tiny Mrs. Langley at the Chester Fritz Library.

We asked Mrs. Langley if she knew anything about Bobby Swenson and his family because she looked to be around the same age Bobby would be if he had lived. Mrs. Langley said that she and her retired Air Force husband had been in Grand Forks for fifteen years, but she knew nothing at all about the Swensons.

"I can show you a good tool to use, though," she said and led us to an open computer. She logged on to an Internet search engine that I had never heard of before, explaining that the library had a subscription to use it. "It's usually pretty good at tracking down people and other information," Mrs. Langley said. She wished us luck and moved on to help another patron.

Aggie sat down at the keyboard. "Let's test this out," she said. She typed in her last name and her mom's first name—Elizabeth—and sure enough, the system responded with her address and phone number right on UND's campus. "Pretty good," Aggie agreed. "We're unlisted."

"What about your dad?" I asked out of curiosity. I had only met her mom when we picked up the twins for our sleepover.

"What about him?" Aggie responded defensively. Her eyes narrowed and she stared at me darkly for a long moment. It was a look I hadn't seen before.

"Sorry," I said. "I was just wondering—"

"It's okay," she said, becoming her usual self again. "I'm sorry. We just don't talk much about him, that's all."

Here was another mystery, but I knew better than to ask Aggie anything else about it at that time. "Try *Swenson*," I said. The system responded with three RJ Swensons: one in Florida, one in New York, and one in Minnesota. Aggie printed out all of the listings, but we both had a hunch that the Minnesota address was our best bet because it was right next door to North Dakota. Aggie flipped open a spiral notebook and together we came up with a list of possibilities:

- The Swensons live in one of the three locations we found online; or
- They live somewhere else, possibly even in North Dakota, but keep their identity a secret; or
- One or both of them are already dead.

As we walked out of the library, Aggie and I were feeling pleased with ourselves for being so thorough, and we knew that Mandy and Alex would be impressed as well. But then it suddenly hit me that we hadn't thought about our next step.

"What do we do now?" I asked. I held a pretend phone to my ear. "Hi, Mr. Swenson? Sorry to hear about your son getting killed fifty years ago. Oh, and by the way, did you push him?"

Aggie chuckled. "I guess that does sound kind of . . . pushy," she observed, and we both laughed. We decided that we would need a full meeting of the twins to decide how to proceed. We went to the basketball court to kill some time because we knew it would be a while before Mandy and Alex returned from their assignment. Red River High was far enough away that they had to take a bus. Aggie and I shot two games of around-the-world, but our hearts weren't in it; we were too excited about the whole Swenson case.

When we returned to the quadrangle, we found that the other twins were as excited as we were. They came racing over to us carrying a hardbound book. They said that the secretary had been incredibly nice to them and let them borrow the school's copy of the 1964-1965 yearbook.

"The lady actually got choked up when she was talking about Bobby," Mandy said. "She went to school with him right through eleventh grade."

"What did you say, exactly, to get the conversation rolling?" I asked.

"Pretty much the truth," Alex said. "We told her that Mandy was staying out at Foxtrot-Zero and heard that Bobby lost his life there in an accident."

"I said that I just wanted to learn more about him," Mandy added.

"You didn't say anything about the ghost or spirit or whatever, did you?" Aggie prodded. I wondered the same thing.

"No way," Alex snorted. "She'd probably think we were nuts or something."

"Hey, if the shell fits . . . ," I quipped. Only Aggie laughed.

"Here, check this out," Mandy said and opened the front cover of the yearbook. There was a full-page, color photograph of a teenager in a varsity jacket with leather sleeves. He had slicked-back blond hair, smoky blue eyes, and a kind of restless smile. "Who does he look like?" Mandy challenged me. "Come on."

"Like James Dean," I observed.

"Exactly!" Mandy exclaimed.

Aggie and Alex weren't sure who we were talking about, so I explained that James Dean was a cool young actor back in the 1950s. "Our parents own a movie of his called *Rebel Without a Cause*," I continued. "After watching it a couple of times, I had to agree with what my father always says: James Dean was the coolest."

"Yeah, and all the girls were crazy about him," Mandy chimed in. "Too bad he died in a car accident when he was just in his twenties."

"We'll need to get that *Rebel* movie from the library," Aggie said as we all stared at Bobby's picture.

Yes, it sure looked like Bobby was the Grand Forks, North Dakota, version of James Dean. His dedication page read, "In loving memory of Bobby Swenson, 1948-1964. Excellent student, outstanding athlete, capable leader, and friend to all. You will be missed."

"Did you happen to ask where Bobby's parents live these days?" I asked.

Alex nodded. "All the secretary knew was that they moved somewhere out of state right after Bobby's funeral."

"Probably to start living it up on the fifty thousand dollars," Mandy concluded, shaking her head in disgust. "That's a lot of money now, but fifty years ago it was like being rich."

Seeing that dedication page gave me an idea for how to approach Bobby's parents if we managed to contact them. We could say that we were doing a research project on the history of Grand Forks when we came across Bobby's story. To honor him, we would like to place a memorial marker of some kind outside Foxtrot-Zero.

"And that could be true," Aggie said after I explained my idea. "We could actually do it."

"We could use these same words," Mandy said and nodded toward the yearbook dedication. I thought that was a great plan.

"First let's see if we have any luck with the picture," Alex said.

*******

We all went with my mom to the Burkes' dormitory apartment to see about another sleepover. The apartment was nice—tidy, as my mom put it—but also cramped. Four twins and two adults just barely fit in the living room. Ms. Burke (I had called her *Mrs.* Burke, but she corrected me) gave my mom a cup of coffee while Aggie and Alex went to their bedrooms to get their things.

"I'd like to take a turn and have your twins for a sleepover sometime," Ms. Burke said. "As you can see, we're a little short on space, but we'll make do." Ms. Burke was younger than my mom, but she had a tired look about her. "I started sleeping out here on the pull-out bed last year because we only have two bedrooms. The twins are at that age now where they need their own space, you know?"

"I *do* know," Mom assured her.

"It's tough to provide with just my income and trying to finish my college degree and all," Ms. Burke confided.

"Well, it seems to me you're providing very nicely," Mom said, and I was proud of her for saying that. "Both of your kids are just wonderful."

"Thank you," Ms. Burke said with a smile that brightened her face and made her look suddenly younger. Then she added, quietly, "They're about the only thing my ex-husband ever did right in his entire life."

We all pretended not to hear that. Mandy and I stared at a "Joe Blanchard for Senate" ad on TV while our mom just sipped her coffee. I would hate for anyone to say something like that about my father, and I felt sad for Aggie and Alex. I actually avoided making eye contact with either of them on our way to Foxtrot-Zero.

# CHAPTER EIGHT

After eating cooked-out hamburgers and hotdogs, we all played a game of hide-and-seek in the sunflower fields surrounding Foxtrot-Zero. Even my parents played! Those sunflowers really did grow a few inches every day. I crouched down in a cluster of them and felt like I was alone in the world, and then suddenly, *whack*! Someone would slap me on the shoulder and scream, "Gotcha!" The game was fun but kind of nerve-wracking.

"Ollie-ollie oxen free!" Dad finally called out. "The mosquitoes are getting too vicious."

You wouldn't believe the size of mosquitoes in North Dakota. The townspeople joke about how the mosquito is the state bird, and they even tell stories about pairs of them swooping down and carrying away pets and small children.

"They pick them up by the ears like this," my father insisted and pulled on my ears as we entered the aboveground house.

"Yeah, right!" I said.

"You can believe what you want to believe," Dad teased.

He was in a great mood, so I knew his writing must have gone extremely well that day. I decided this was a good time to ask if we twins could head down to the capsule again. "I promise we won't break anything," I said.

"I'm not worried about that," Dad said. "And I was only upset last time because I didn't know where you guys were.

That was a crummy feeling, especially because your mom and I were responsible for the other twins' safety as well. What do you plan on doing down there anyway?"

"Just watch TV and stuff," Mandy said.

"Does the 'stuff' include a spinning bottle?" Dad asked and danced his eyebrows up and down.

"Daddy!" Mandy said and slapped him on the chest. Alex pushed his glasses up on his nose and blushed, which was hard for him to disguise with that pasty complexion of his.

"It's just a cool place to hang out, Mr. C.," Aggie said. "Kind of like an underground tree fort."

"Underground tree fort," Dad repeated. "That's a pretty good analogy, Aggie. You should be a writer."

*******

The song "Come a Little Bit Closer" greeted us as we entered the capsule. "Poor Bobby must play that CD twenty-four/seven!" I observed. Alex turned down the volume and dimmed the lights, and then we got into our familiar circle on the floor. Mandy lit the candle once again. We were trying to set ourselves up exactly as we had been the last time. We figured that if it had worked once, it should work again.

I still felt nervous about the whole situation, but now I was more curious than scared. After seeing Bobby's picture, I began thinking about him as a real person who died when he was only five years older than us twins. If his energy or spirit was still around and needed help of some kind, I guessed we would be his best hope.

"Bobby, it's us again," Alex began. "We're glad you enjoy the music, and now we have another little present for you. It's the Red River High yearbook from your junior year."

"You were an amazing guy, Bobby," Mandy said. "Look at what your classmates did for you." She held the book in her lap and opened to the dedication page. "See? It's in color and everything. All the other pictures are black and white."

"We're hoping that you can see this picture and that it will help you show yourself to us," Alex said.

"We want to be able to communicate with you better," I said. Everyone looked at me because it was the first time I had said anything directly to Bobby. I suddenly felt more at ease, like when I was in the sixth-grade play at school. I had almost barfed when I walked out onto the stage and saw how many people were in the audience, but as soon as I delivered my first line, I was okay.

We sat there for a while bathed in the soft glow from above and the electrical hum from below. Nothing was happening. And then Bobby gave us a little hint: The music skipped back to the beginning of "Come a Little Bit Closer." The song played for about ten seconds and then skipped back to the beginning, over and over again.

"I've got it!" Alex yelled, startling all of us. "He wants the yearbook over by the ka-chunker machine. That must be where he feels most comfortable."

That sounded reasonable to all of us, so we got up and walked over to that communications rack. Now the song played on normally in the background. Drawing on my new courage, I took the book from Mandy and held Bobby's picture in front of the little window.

"Bobby, can you become yourself again and talk to us?" I asked. I couldn't believe I was speaking those words!

The machine started *ka-chunking* in response. It took a ridiculously long time for each word to print out as I looked through the illuminated window:

OSCAR NOVEMBER LIMA

## YANKEE SIERRA ECHO
## ECHO

"What's he saying?" everyone was asking.

"O-N-L-Y-S-E-E," I said. "Only see."

"Oh man, it'll take forever talking this way," Aggie complained.

"I've got it!" Alex yelled again. And once again, the rest of us jumped.

"Stop doing that!" Mandy scolded and slapped Alex. "You're gonna give us all heart attacks."

"Well, then we'd really be able to communicate with Bobby on his own level," I said, trying to toss in a little humor. "Assuming we all croaked, I mean."

"Okay, now listen," Alex said excitedly. His eyes were dazzling. "Here's the thing: Bobby is pure energy now, right? So rather than just show him a picture, let's feed it in to him digitally."

"What?" I asked suspiciously.

"I saw upstairs that your dad has a document scanner," Alex explained. "So here's what we do: We scan Bobby's picture and then feed the image directly into the old computer down here. Bobby should be able to tap into that because a digital image is nothing but energy too, just like him."

"Where's the computer down here?" I asked. There was a metal keyboard bolted to the commander's console, but I didn't know where the actual computer was.

"We were sitting right by it in our circle," Alex said matter-of-factly. "There's a rack labeled Launch Control Facility Processor, and one of the panels on that rack says Memory Controller Group. That's got to be the computer's hard drive. Even though it's really old, I'm sure I can rig a cable to communicate with it."

"You can do that?" Mandy asked.

"Trust me, he can do anything with computers," Aggie said proudly.

Mandy picked up the phone and dialed our topside phone number. "Daddy, can we come up and borrow your scanner and extra laptop for a little while?" She wrapped the cord around her finger while she talked.

*Not just the cord*, I was thinking.

# CHAPTER NINE

"Just please don't break anything," my father said when we told him we wanted his spare laptop to play a new game that Alex was showing us. Naturally, Dad had two computers in case one crashed on him. He has been in love with the idea of "redundant systems"—having a backup for everything—since his Air Force days. Dad even relies on a redundant system for waking up each morning: If his clock radio loses power or breaks in the middle of the night, his Little Ben windup alarm clock stands ready to spring into action and save the day.

Alex is a genius when it comes to computers, and there's no other way to put it. Back down in the capsule, Alex used a pair of needle-nose pliers to work on the end of a cable and then said, "There!" Sure enough, he had set up communications between the laptop and the ancient military computer. He managed to download the digital image of sixteen-year-old Bobby without blowing anything up, so Dad had nothing to worry about.

"That's it?" I asked.

"That should do it," Alex responded confidently, sounding like the guy who works on our air conditioner every summer back home.

Alex made Bobby's picture the wallpaper image on the laptop, so we all just stood in a circle and stared at the screen. In the silence I became aware again of the electrical hum; it felt like it was enfolding me in its arms. I had a nice, buzzy feeling like I was about to nod off to sleep. My mind drifted to Sarah Beasley. *Who are you with at this exact moment? Who's lucky enough to be with you? If I fell into a seventy-foot pit, would you even care?*

"Do we need to get the candle going and everything?" Aggie asked, breaking the spell I was under.

"I was hoping we were past all that by now," Mandy responded, and we all looked to Alex for an answer.

"I'm not sure what to tell you," he said in frustration. "The electronic image is floating around in the capsule's computer—that much is for sure. Maybe Bobby just hasn't located it yet."

*Ka-chunk, ka-chunk.* Mandy got to the communications rack first and dropped to her knees.

"What is it?" the rest of us asked impatiently. "What's he saying?"

"What's he *drawing* is more like it," Mandy replied and continued staring into the little window.

"Drawing?" I repeated and tried to wedge myself in beside Mandy.

"Just hold on!" she shouted and refused to give up her position.

After another minute of ka-chunking, Mandy pressed the Advance button and tore off the paper. What she held up for us to see was a black and white version of the yearbook picture that Alex had scanned. We all laughed in amazement, but soon Alex pursed his lips and shook his head.

"What's the problem?" I asked. "This is Bobby's way of showing us that he found your file!"

"Yeah," Alex said and slowly pushed up his glasses. "But it's also Bobby's way of showing that this is the best he can do with the file."

We all groaned. "So he can't, like, materialize and talk to us?" I asked Alex. "I thought you said—"

"Apparently I wasn't a hundred percent correct then," Alex snapped, avoiding the expression "I was wrong."

"I'm sure Alex did his best," Aggie said in support of her brother.

"I'm sure he did," I reassured both Burke twins. "I'm just saying that this ka-chunking stuff takes forever."

"If you have a better idea, then let's hear it," Alex taunted.

"Sorry to offend you, Boy Genius," I said dramatically.

"You know what?" Alex began with a red face.

"Just stop it, you two!" Mandy warned, sounding exactly like our mother.

"Why don't you do something useful?" Alex continued, addressing me. "Like reenacting another one of your world-famous chess matches. Maybe someday you'll actually learn how to play a decent game on your own."

"Drop it!" Aggie yelled, looking from Alex to me.

I locked eyes with Alex, getting steamed. "Speaking of playing, why don't you get your pasty white butt out in the sun at least once a year to play basketball or something?"

Alex moved in so close to me that our noses were almost touching. "How about—" he began. His words were halted when two old magazines suddenly flew off the commander's console and hit each of us on the shoulder. The impact didn't hurt, but it did startle us.

"Whoa!" we both exclaimed.

"That's Bobby telling you two to stop acting like babies," Mandy announced with great importance, as though Alex and I hadn't already figured that out.

"Yeah, give it a rest," Aggie added. She looked disgusted to be within five feet of us.

My face must have turned as red as Alex's was now. I was embarrassed for behaving like a preschooler in front of both Aggie—my basketball buddy—and a cool teenager like Bobby. I looked at the laptop screen, half expecting that James Dean figure to turn his head in disgust.

"Sorry," I said quietly. Even though this word of apology was aimed at Aggie and Bobby, Alex sheepishly held his hand out to me. "Me too," he said, and we shook on it.

"Okay, now let's get refocused," Mandy ordered. "We'll see if we can get any useful information from Bobby, even if we have to stick with the old-fashioned ka-chunking method."

Aggie opened her spiral notebook, ready to record our questions and Bobby's responses. We sat down on the floor in front of the ka-chunker and made eye contact with the window as though it was Bobby's face.

"You said you were pushed into the pit back in 1964, Bobby," Mandy began. "Do you know who did it?"

NOVEMBER        OSCAR—"No"—was        Bobby's response.

"We need a lead to help us find out who did this to you," I said, still feeling a little awkward addressing an invisible force. "Can you tell us who on the construction site may have wanted to hurt you?"

I wondered if Bobby knew anything about the insurance policy, but I didn't want to be the one to bring it up. My stomach did flip-flops as the *ka-chunking* began. Bobby's response had nothing to do with his father, though; the message decoded to "Karl Henderson."

"Why this Karl Henderson guy?" Alex asked. "What did he have against you?"

Bobby's reply took at least two minutes to print out and decoded to "My father just fired his son Frank."

"Okay! Now we're getting somewhere," Mandy declared.

"Is there anyone else you can think of at this time, Bobby?" I prodded.

NOVEMBER OSCAR.

"One more question for you before we go," Mandy began. "If your parents moved to one of these three states—Florida, New York, or Minnesota—which one would it be?" Mandy sounded like a game show host posing a multiple-choice question. I could picture Bobby hunched over a contestant's stand, reasoning through each of the choices.

MIKE NOVEMBER.

"MN: That's the abbreviation for Minnesota," Aggie said. She was so organized; I saw her flip back a few pages in her notebook and circle *Minnesota* on the list we'd made. She wrote *#1* next to it.

"I wish we could make that ka-chunker print a whole lot faster," Mandy said as we prepared to head topside.

"Even better would be if Bobby could instant-message us on the laptop," I added, just thinking out loud.

"Hold on a second!" Alex shouted. *Here we go again,* I was thinking. *Boy Genius at work.*

Alex's plan was to write what he called a "parsing program" on the laptop. It would take whatever messages Bobby fed into the ka-chunker and quickly assemble them as complete sentences on the laptop. Alex's theory was that communicating with Bobby was slow only because the printer was slow and because the ka-chunker was designed to print out each letter of the alphabet as a whole word: ALPHA, BRAVO, CHARLIE, and so on.

"Think about it," Alex said, all fired up. "Since Bobby is pure energy, he could communicate at . . . at virtually the speed of light!"

Alex definitely held our attention now. "How long would it take you to write a program like that?" Mandy asked.

"Not sure. Could take hours, I guess," Alex said. He said that the goal would be to turn off the ka-chunker's printer and allow Bobby's words to flow onto the laptop screen. "Just like instant messaging," Alex concluded, giving me a friendly pat on the shoulder.

"For sure that wouldn't blow up my dad's computer or anything, right?" I asked.

"Absolutely not," Alex replied quickly and confidently. Then, after a few seconds, "Most likely not."

"Oh, great," I scoffed.

"It's a chance we'll have to take," Mandy said with a mischievous smile.

"Yeah?" I said. "Well, I'll leave it to you to smooth things over with *Daddy* if something goes wrong."

Alex disconnected the laptop and we made our way toward the blast door. "See you later!" we called out to Bobby. When we got to the kitchenette, we heard the *ka-chunking* begin once again.

"Hey, I wonder what that's about," Mandy said.

"He's probably just saying 'Bye,'" I offered.

We couldn't resist, though. We went back to find a long message scrolling out of the ka-chunker's print slot. It took forever.

"Man, you'd better get started right away on that program of yours," I advised Alex.

Eventually, Bobby's message decoded to, "More music on little record, please. Little Deuce Coupe by Beach Boys."

"Little record?" Aggie repeated.

"Oh, I get it!" I said. "He wants us to score him another CD to listen to. It's called a compact disc, Bobby—a CD. We'll find the one you want."

"Poor guy," Mandy said. "He must be sick of the CD he already has down here."

"One CD with five songs on it isn't a whole lot to keep you company," Aggie agreed. "It must get so lonely."

# CHAPTER TEN

Now that we had a couple of important leads to follow, the four of us decided to work together rather than dividing up responsibilities. We wanted to make sure we didn't mess anything up. The next day on campus we waited until Ms. Burke left to do grocery shopping, and then we set up for a phone call in the living room. Aggie placed a speakerphone and an old, pocket-sized cassette recorder on the coffee table. She sat next to me on the couch and began dialing. Mandy and Alex sat across from us on the loveseat.

I had been elected by the rest of the twins to handle this phone call. We all decided that it would be best to have just one person talk so that the Swensons didn't feel like people were ganging up on them. "Why me?" I asked nervously.

"Because you're the one who came up with the idea about the memorial," Mandy reminded me. She reached across the coffee table and patted my knee. Mandy was right, of course, but now I wasn't sure what we were hoping to accomplish. I couldn't very well ask Mr. Swenson if he had pushed his son or what he and his wife had done with the life insurance money. I also couldn't ask what he knew about a guy named Karl Henderson "because, by the way, your son's spirit energy singled out Karl as a suspect in his death." This would sound really crazy to the Swensons. It sounded that way to me too. I figured the best

I could do was nose around and see if anything useful came out of the conversation.

Aggie pointed at the speakerphone. The Swensons' line was ringing, and I swear my heart was pounding out three beats to each ring. Aggie pressed the Record button and the cassette tape whirred to life. I was hoping that the line would keep on ringing or that just voicemail would pick up. No such luck.

"Hello," a woman's gentle voice answered.

"Hello, Mrs. Swenson?" I said trying to sound like a nice kid so she would know I wasn't a telemarketer. Even my Grandma Cousineau hangs up on telemarketers and she's one of the friendliest people in the world.

"Yes?"

"My name is Mark Cousineau and I'm calling from Grand Forks, North Dakota."

Just silence on the other end.

"Ma'am, are you still there?" I asked.

"What is this about?" Mrs. Swenson asked suspiciously.

"A few other students and I are doing a project about local history and we decided to create a memorial to honor Bobby. It would be placed along the road by Foxtrot-Zero."

Again, just silence. I felt my face get hot. This phone conversation seemed to be pretty one-sided.

"Hello?" I said timidly.

"Who is this?" a man's voice suddenly boomed through the speaker. I almost ran out of the room, I was so shaken. I was stone silent for a few moments, but the other twins mouthed the words "Go on" and pumped their fists in the air. I was sure my face was beet red now.

"I'm sorry to disturb you, sir," I said and again repeated what I had told Mrs. Swenson. And then I added, "I *am* talking to the right Mr. and Mrs. Swenson, aren't I—Bobby's parents?"

"Yes you are, young man," Mr. Swenson said, sounding more at ease. I used the back of my hand to wipe sweat from my forehead. "I think you can imagine that we're taken by surprise here," Mr. Swenson continued. "I mean, it's been fifty years since the accident."

"I know. It's been a long time," I said.

"Although sometimes it still feels like it was just yesterday," Mr. Swenson added.

"You still think about him a lot, sir?" I asked.

"How could I not? Bobby was our only child and he was a great one, let me tell you. His teachers loved him, his coaches loved him, and pretty much everyone else loved him too because he was such a good person all-around. So full of life." Mr. Swenson was getting choked up, and I was ready to wind up the call. I felt sorry for him.

"He must have been really special, Mr. Swenson," I said. "My friends and I saw the dedication page in Red River's yearbook and that's how we got the idea for a memorial."

"Well, that's very kind of you to help keep Bobby's memory alive. That's something his mother and I do by thinking about him every day. And by offering a scholarship in his name."

"A scholarship?" I repeated. This sounded interesting.

"That's right," Mr. Swenson said. "When Bobby died he had a life insurance policy for fifty thousand dollars." The other twins leaned in closer to the speaker phone.

"Wow—fifty thousand dollars!" I exclaimed, pretending this was news to me. "If you don't mind my asking, why did a young kid have such a big life insurance policy? Was Bobby ill or something?"

"No, not at all," Mr. Swenson replied patiently. "We bought the policy to help out a neighbor of ours who sold insurance and was having a hard time making ends meet for his family."

"That was very nice of you," I said. Mandy shrugged her shoulders, and then she and Aggie nodded their heads. I could tell they believed Mr. Swenson's story. Alex, however, rocked his hand back and forth to show that the old man's story sounded a little fishy to him.

"Well, when Bobby passed away, his mother and I didn't want one red cent of that money, so we donated it all to Minnesota State University here in Mankato," Mr. Swenson explained.

"That's a lot of money," I observed.

"Especially back then," he agreed. "And based on how the university invested it, they're still able to offer a scholarship each year in Bobby's name. It's for an incoming freshman who goes into the pre-law program because that's what Bobby wanted to do."

"What a great idea!" I said sincerely.

"You sound pretty young, Mark," Mr. Swenson said. "But when you're college age you might want to consider applying for this scholarship if it interests you. Since you're from North Dakota, no doubt you can handle the winters here." He chuckled.

I thanked Mr. Swenson for the offer and didn't bother to explain that I was actually from Ohio. Mr. Swenson ended the conversation by apologizing for his rough tone when he'd first taken the phone. He told me that I should feel free to call again if I needed any information for the memorial. "Mrs. Swenson and I might even consider coming out to Grand Forks for the dedication," he said. "That would be our first time there in fifty years. We're eighty-six years old, though, so don't hold your breath waiting for us!"

After I clicked off the phone, Aggie rewound the tape and we listened to the whole conversation over again to make sure we hadn't missed anything. We hadn't; Mr. Swenson just sounded like someone who would make a terrific great-grandpa.

"First of all," Mandy began, "the Swensons seem like nice people who still miss their son after fifty years."

"And the fact that the scholarship exists means that they didn't use the insurance money for anything selfish," I concluded.

Aggie made a note that Mr. Swenson was no longer a prime suspect in his son's murder case.

"But we can't rule out that maybe Mr. Swenson *did* do it and planned to buy a new house or something with the money," Alex said. "And then he and his wife started feeling too guilty about the whole thing, and that's when they came up with the scholarship idea."

"No way!" I protested.

"I'm not saying I think this is true," Alex responded. "But I *am* saying we shouldn't totally cross out the Swensons at this point."

The rest of us reluctantly agreed that what Alex said was possible, but not probable. We decided to focus our attention next on Karl Henderson, the construction worker whose son Mr. Swenson had fired before Bobby's fall.

We found a listing in the local phonebook for Frank Henderson, but not for Karl. This caused us to stop and do a little math. We figured that a man with a nineteen-year-old son in 1964 must have been around forty back then. That would make him ninety now. Even though the Swensons sounded like they were in good health, we knew that not everyone is that fortunate when it comes to lifespan. In other words, Karl may have died years ago.

Mrs. Langley at the library told us about the County Recorder's office, a place where we could sort through obituaries—death notices—for as far back as records have been kept. She said that this would be a lot more efficient than just looking through old copies of *The Grand Forks Herald* and hoping we found the right one.

An old man named Mr. Chomsky took care of us at the County Recorder's office. From his ghostly white complexion—whiter even than Alex's—you would guess that he hadn't left the records room for even a moment during the past three decades. But at least he retained a sense of humor; he laughed when we asked for the obituary listings. I suppose it's unusual for kids to be interested in that kind of thing.

"Do you have a parent with you?" he asked, smiling.

"No, just us," Aggie replied. "We'll be real careful with your records, though."

"May I ask whose obituary you're looking for exactly?" he asked suspiciously.

I was tempted to say "Yours!" But I doubt that Mr. Chomsky's sense of humor would have extended that far. Fortunately, Mandy piped up instead. "Mr. Karl Henderson's," she said.

"And may I ask why?" Mr. Chomsky prodded.

"Sir, are we required to give you all these details?" Alex boldly asked. "Isn't there something called the Freedom of Information Act? We would just like to look through the county obituaries. Please."

Alex's face went from pasty white to tomato red as he locked eyes with Mr. Chomsky. Mr. Chomsky cracked first. "Okay, okay," he laughed. "I would normally insist on having an adult in here with you, but I'm afraid this one"— he nodded at Alex—"would have a lawyer knocking at my door tomorrow. Unless he's already a lawyer himself. Who knows?"

Wow, was I ever impressed with Alex! Mr. Chomsky led us into a small, musty room and showed us how to search through the records. When he left us alone it didn't take long to find a listing for Karl Henderson. His obituary said that he had died in 1997 at the age of seventy-three. He was identified as husband of the late Gertrude Hanscom-Henderson, which meant that his wife had died before him. Well, if Karl had something to do with pushing Bobby he took that information to the grave with him. Unless, of course, he had shared anything with his son Frank, who was listed among his surviving children and grandchildren.

"Come again soon," Mr. Chomsky said as we prepared to leave. "Just leave your pit bull at home next time," he chuckled.

When we got outside I patted Alex's head and said, "Good boy!"

"Oh, shut up!" he said with a laugh.

Aggie put her hands around Alex's throat. "Now I know what Mom and I are getting you for our next birthday: a new collar!"

"Ha-ha," Alex said, getting fed up. "Anyone else want to make fun of me?" he asked, looking at Mandy.

"I think you did great in there," Mandy said seriously and gave him a quick hug. Alex pushed up his glasses and smiled as though he'd just won a major award.

We decided we had done enough sleuthing for one day; our Frank Henderson lead would have to wait. Off we went to Columbia Mall for an ice cream cone and to look for the Beach Boys CD that Bobby requested. Between walking and taking busses, Mandy and I were really getting to know our way around town. Aggie and Alex led the way, of course, but we were paying attention and we liked what we saw. I began to understand why our mom and dad had become so attached to Grand Forks as newlyweds.

*******

Later that day, the four of us were seated on the Burkes' living room floor watching *Rebel Without a Cause*. The girls had taken the tunnel over to the Chester Fritz Library after our trip to the mall and found a copy of it on DVD.

"I need to see that part over again," Alex said excitedly. He briefly rewound the scene and pressed Play. "You're tearing me apart!" James Dean's character, Jim Stark, howled once again. Jim is a troubled teenager who has been hauled off to the local police station for public intoxication, and his words of anguish are hurled in the direction of his bickering parents and grandmother.

"That's an awesome line!" Alex said and paused the movie. Jim's face, all scrunched up in pain and anger, pretty much filled the screen now.

"Yeah, I'm glad you told us about this," Aggie added. "That James Dean guy was a great actor."

Mandy and I looked at each other with pride, as though we had just introduced the twins to our favorite older cousin, and now they thought he was as cool as we did.

In the movie, Jim is the new kid in town; his family has moved once again to try to keep him out of trouble. The so-called teenagers at his new high school look way too old to be there. Everyone smokes cigarettes, and no one, except an awkward kid named Plato, is nice to Jim. Even Jim's pretty next-door neighbor, Judy, is mean. One of the very first things she says to him is, "I'll bet you're a real yo-yo." But Jim plays it off real cool, shooting back with, "I love you too." We twins had a good laugh at that line.

"It's really stupid the way Judy treats him, though," Mandy proclaimed. "Doesn't she notice that he's, like, gorgeous?"

Alex and I just rolled our eyes. I think it sounds so phony when girls use the word *gorgeous* to describe a guy. Anyway, Judy does eventually fall for Jim, and when he kisses her for the first time on the forehead, she says dreamily, "Your lips are soft." Mandy and Aggie both sighed.

The movie isn't just a love story, though; there's plenty of action. For example, when bullies pick on Jim and call him a chicken, he winds up in a knife fight. He also agrees to compete against the head bully, Buzz Gunderson, in a *chickie run*. A chickie run involves racing stolen cars toward the edge of a high cliff, and whoever bails out of his car first is the chicken. Jim wears a high-collared red jacket in that scene, looking too cool for even Death himself to handle.

I could picture Bobby Swenson in that red jacket, and I wondered if maybe he was wearing one similar to that on the day he died. Poor Bobby. When Jim Stark made the decisions to take part in a knife fight and a chickie run, he had to realize he was risking his life. The only decision Bobby made on his last day was to deliver his father's lunch to him at the Foxtrot-Zero construction site. He was just being a good son. I wondered, Did *he* leave behind a girl who thought his lips were soft?

# CHAPTER ELEVEN

"Ready for countdown," Alex announced confidently the next day, pointing the cursor at a Download button on the laptop screen. The four of us were huddled in the capsule, ready to test Alex's parsing program. The Burke twins had spent another night with us at Foxtrot-Zero, and poor Alex had devoted many of those hours to writing and revising his program. Now the cable was connected between the laptop and the capsule's ancient computer—the Memory Controller Group—and all that remained was a click of the mouse.

I held hands with Aggie and Mandy in nervous anticipation. "Three, two, one . . . click!" I said. *Please don't blow up my father's laptop,* I was thinking. It was, in fact, the Fourth of July, but I wasn't interested in experiencing fireworks in an underground capsule.

We stared at the screen, hoping our mental powers would prod the download into moving a little faster. It didn't work. The progress bar moved about a millimeter every ten seconds, and I swear our hands were so hot you could use the sweat to slick back your hair for a week.

"It's locked up," Alex said quietly after about ten minutes.

"What?" I protested. "I thought you were sure this—"

"Just hold on," he muttered. Alex rebooted the laptop and brought us to the brink of another countdown. "Let Mandy say it this time," Alex ordered.

"Oh, right," I snickered. "Like it's really gonna matter who counts backwards from three. For a smart guy, you're pretty superstitious."

"Let Mandy say it," Alex repeated, glaring at me. His eyes were bloodshot from lack of sleep and his hair was sticking up every which way. *Mad scientist . . . mad Boy Genius,* I thought to myself.

"Three, two, one . . . click!" Mandy said. Sure enough, the progress bar moved across the screen smoothly this time, centimeter by centimeter.

Aggie started to wriggle her hand free from mine. "Don't jinx us," I said and clamped tighter.

Alex smirked. "So much for Mr. Anti-Superstition," he baited me.

"Download complete!" Mandy happily announced before I had a chance to respond to Alex.

The laptop screen indicated that Alex's program had found a home in the Memory Controller Group, and without blowing anything up. We finally released our cramped, sweaty hands.

"Now to see how this works!" Alex said with excitement. He removed the cable from the capsule's computer and then used it to connect the laptop to the ka-chunker. "Bobby, we're gonna shut off the switch on the ka-chunker's printer. When you want to say something to us, just do it how you normally do, and we should be able to get it on our computer screen. Okay?"

Alex nodded at me and I shut off the printer switch he was talking about.

"Okay, say something, Bobby!" Mandy commanded.

Again, we were all frozen, staring at the screen. After a short delay, the following message scrolled smoothly onto the screen: what did you find out about karl henderson

"Oh, man!" we cried out and gave each other high-fives.

"Unfortunately, Karl Henderson died years ago," Mandy informed Bobby.

"But we're not giving up," Aggie assured him. "We'll track down his son Frank tomorrow and see what he knows."

thank you

"This beats waiting for messages to print out of the ka-chunker," I observed.

not kachunker survivable low frequency communications system they called it the slifix for short

"He must be talking about the missile crewmembers who used to be down here," Mandy explained to the Burke twins. "Like our dad."

As if on cue, Dad called down to the capsule on the phone line. "Time to get moving," he said. We would be dropping off the Burkes and staying in town for a family day.

"Sorry, Bobby," I said. "We have to leave for now."

"Just when it's getting good," Aggie protested, like a little girl who's being pulled out of a movie theater.

Another message appeared on the screen: music please

"The Beach Boys!" Mandy exclaimed.

"Doesn't your program do capital letters or punctuation?" I innocently asked Alex. He just stared at me in response. With his wild hair and wild eyes, he looked as though he would have enjoyed nothing better than to strangle me. "Sorry," I quickly added.

It took a minute of serious work for me to open the CD. "Got it!" I said proudly when the deed was done. I always feel like I've won a game of Bingo or something whenever I finish peeling the plastic wrap from a CD case. And now I was trying to shake the wrap off my hand. A lot of static electricity builds up in an underground capsule.

`side one please`

"Everything's on one side," Mandy said and held the CD toward the slifix.

`strange`

The first song on the CD was the title cut, "Little Deuce Coupe," which was about a fast car. I looked through the CD insert and quickly discovered that most Beach Boys songs were about cars, girls, or surfing—or some combination of those three. We started to listen to another upbeat song called "Be True to Your School," but Dad interrupted with a phone call. "Let's *go!*" he barked. I knew that any further words he spoke would be through gritted teeth, so we hurried off toward the blast door.

"See ya, Bobby," we called out. "Happy Fourth!" Aggie added.

*******

"Ooo, I like those spaghetti ones the best!" Mom exclaimed as a rocket from the fireworks display burst into long strands of stardust.

I looked at my watch and held my hand out to Mandy. She reluctantly pulled a dollar bill from her purse and gave it to me.

"Thanks a lot, Mom," Mandy whined. "I just lost a dollar because of you."

"What are you talking about?" Mom asked.

"I bet Mandy you'd say the spaghetti thing within ten minutes after the fireworks started," I said, sticking the bill in my pocket. "You do it every year."

"So sor-*ry* I'm getting predictable in my old age," Mom said, pretending that her feelings were hurt.

"I love you just the way you are," Dad crooned softly and snuggled in closer to Mom. Mandy and I groaned and looked around to make sure no one had overheard our lame parents.

All clear. What caught my attention, though, was a boyfriend-girlfriend couple seated on a blanket near ours. They were just kids, like maybe a year older than Mandy and me. I could see the boy's hand on the girl's shoulder, but his arm was completely covered by her long brown hair as they tilted their heads skyward. I thought it would be so cool to be with a girl all alone at a fireworks display . . . or at the movies . . . or anywhere for that matter. But then again, what would happen if you ran out of things to say after about ten minutes? I mean, wouldn't it be embarrassing if you thought you really liked a girl and got all amped up about going out with her, and then you totally ran out of things to say?

I wondered what Sarah Beasley was doing back in Cleveland Heights at that exact moment. Mandy leaned in toward me. "Missing someone?" she teased. It's kind of cool and kind of annoying how well we can read each other's thoughts at times.

"Shut up," I said for old time's sake, but I didn't really mean it. Mandy and I had been getting along incredibly well ever since we'd teamed up to work on Bobby's case.

"You think Alex and Aggie are watching fireworks?" Mandy asked. The Burkes had gone down to Fargo, about an hour away, for an overnight stay with some cousins.

"Maybe," I replied absently. Hearing Aggie's name caused me to wonder what *she* was doing at that exact moment. And then this question hit me: *If I could choose one girl to share a blanket with right here, right now, would it be Sarah or*

*Aggie?* Maybe I was starting to have a thing for my basketball buddy—my foot-taller-than-me, better-player-than-me, basketball buddy. "Uh-oh," I actually said aloud.

"What 'uh-oh'?" Mandy asked.

"I think some ash from that last rocket is drifting back toward the crowd," I lied.

*******

I was feeling restless that night back at Foxtrot-Zero, probably from a combination of the fireworks, thinking about Sarah and Aggie, and wondering if we would ever be able to help Bobby. So, at about 12:30 AM, I got out of bed and wrote a note:

*Please don't panic, Mom and Dad. I'm in the capsule.*

The last thing I wanted was a repeat performance of my parents searching the grounds for me. I put the note on my pillow, grabbed my chess kit, and tiptoed past the other bedrooms. I made a quick stop in the kitchen to grab a slice of pizza from the fridge. I was nervous about going down to the capsule all alone, so I tried to make a mission out of it. I pretended that Bobby had sent an instant message saying he needed to speak with me—and me alone—ASAP.

The ride down to the capsule was spooky. It seemed like the elevator knew it was after midnight and I was all by myself. The scissor-door rattled more than usual, and the steel cable groaned, "Go back . . . go back." It sounded exactly like that to me.

*Keep cool,* I told myself. I took a couple of bites of pizza and said aloud, real casually, "Yep, I'm on my way to play chess with a dead guy." That seemed to impress the cable, because it went back to its normal squeaks.

"It's just me, Bobby," I announced nervously as I entered the capsule. A sad Beach Boys song, sung *a cappella*, was playing on the boombox. I walked over to the laptop and found `hello mark` on the screen. He knew my name!

"Jeez, this doesn't sound like a typical Beach Boys song," I observed, trying to make casual conversation.

`my favorite song on the album`

I picked up the CD insert and read the lyrics. The song was called "A Young Man Is Gone" and it was about a "daring young star" who died in a car crash. It wrapped up like this:

> Still a young man is gone
> Yet his legend lingers on
> For he died without a cause.
> And they say that he'll
> Be known for evermore
> As the rebel without a cause.

"*Rebel Without a Cause!*" I exclaimed. "We just watched that movie yesterday. You mean the song is about James Dean?"

`yes  james dean`

"You know what's weird? We were thinking that you kind of looked like James Dean."

`i did everything i could to make people think that`

I laughed at Bobby's response.

`what did you find out about frank henderson`

"That hasn't happened yet," I explained. "It's still just nighttime. I couldn't sleep and thought you might want to play some chess."

I set up the board and we started a game. Now that I wasn't so scared anymore, I could appreciate how incredibly cool it was to watch pieces move across the board on their own. A knight is the only piece that can jump over others, so seeing one levitate and glide through the air to its new space was the most amazing thing to me.

I considered telling Bobby that we had talked to his parents, but decided against it. I didn't want to get into the whole life insurance issue, so I tried some more small talk instead. "Hey Bobby, did you have a girlfriend back in 1964?"

`open the yearbook to jennifer franklin junior year`

I found her picture. She had shoulder-length blond hair, bright eyes, and a reserved smile; you saw only a slice of her teeth. It seemed like if you chucked her picture under the chin and said, "Come on now," she couldn't help bursting into a full-blown grin.

"She's really pretty," I said.

`did she go to christmas ball or prom that year`

"What?" I was confused.

`check the pictures for christmas ball and prom`

I looked at couples' pictures for both events, but couldn't find Jennifer Franklin anywhere. I reviewed all of the pictures one more time just to make sure.

"Jennifer didn't go to either one," I announced.

Bobby offered no response. I wondered what he was feeling. If I were him, I would be pleased to see that my girlfriend hadn't moved on to somebody else already. Then again, I would also feel bad for her because I wouldn't want her to miss out on fun things in life. Maybe Bobby was experiencing these mixed feelings.

I stared down at the board, calculating my next move. When I finally looked up, I saw `i loved that girl` on the screen. Seeing those words made me feel so sad for Bobby's loss. "I'm sure she loved you too," I said. Bobby suddenly seemed like an older brother to me, and I wished we could converse more normally.

"Hey, wait a minute!" I said. My father had once shown me how to use a text-to-speech function on the computer. It was designed to read aloud text for people who are visually impaired, but it could definitely help me out in this situation as well. I opened the Control Panel on the screen and found the Speech Properties box. I enabled the text-to-speech function and clicked on the Preview Voice button. "You have selected Microsoft Sam as the computer's default voice," the computer said rather robotically.

"Good enough!" I exclaimed. I was proud that it was me and not Alex who had thought to use the text-to-speech function. "Bobby, try saying hello."

`hello` appeared on the screen, followed immediately by the Microsoft Sam voice saying "hello."

"Ha!" I exclaimed.

"Your move," Bobby said, apparently not too impressed that I had given him a voice.

"Why us?" I asked Bobby after a period of silence. "Why didn't you communicate with people when you had crewmembers in here twenty-four hours a day?"

"I tried," Bobby said. "I tried screaming to them, but no one could hear me. And then after years of being here, I suddenly discovered I could move things."

"That definitely got people's attention," I said. "Including my dad's."

"For some reason, I couldn't move things whenever I wanted. That part has gotten better. Then when you and your friends made contact with me, I also discovered that I could make words print out on the slifix. I don't know why."

As Bobby spoke, I found the courage to ask the really big question on my mind: "What does it feel like being . . . gone?"

"I think this is my problem: I haven't completely moved on yet. I can still feel the imprint of that hand in the middle of my back, and that is what keeps me here. I know God has something more planned for me, but I just can't get to it yet. Or maybe I'm not letting myself get to it. I don't know."

"Sorry," I said.

"It's very difficult being in this condition for so many years," Bobby went on. "It's like... Have you ever found yourself in the haze between being awake and falling asleep, where you suddenly get a jolt in your mind that makes you think, 'Oh yes, *now* I get it'? Only then you can't remember what it was you were trying to understand in the first place. That's kind of what I'm feeling constantly. I'm never settled."

"Oh, that's terrible!" I said. I really did feel sorry for Bobby and I probably should have just dropped the conversation there, but I couldn't help asking another question: "Why the slifix? Why is that rack like your home base?"

"I don't know," he said. "I'm aware of everything within the capsule, but this is my spot. That's just the way it is. We can't possibly know the reason for every little thing in life."

The speech-to-text function isn't designed to show emotion, but it seemed to me that Bobby was becoming frustrated with all my questions. I had a lot more I wanted to ask, but I managed to keep them to myself. For example, I knew that Bobby could move chess pieces and other small objects, but what was the extent of his abilities? I mean, if he wanted to, could he have flung me clear across the capsule? Also, did time pass for him the same way it did for us? Did he ever sleep? If so, did he dream? He mentioned God; was it possible that his soul was already in heaven and that what was left here on Earth was just a trace of his energy, as Mandy and Alex might say?

I didn't dare ask any of these things now. Maybe the timing would feel right during another visit to the capsule, and maybe it would be easier when the other twins were with me as well.

I moved one of my bishops to the center of the board. "Your move, Bobby," I said quietly.

# CHAPTER TWELVE

Even though Aggie and I devoted a lot of time to sleuthing around Grand Forks, we hadn't totally abandoned our basketball careers. The next day we were working our magic in a two-on-two game against a couple of the local boys. We had perfected our alley-oop play where Aggie would lose her man, drive to the board, and leap just as I launched it to her. She would catch the ball in mid-flight and rap it in for a lay-up. *One of these years that girl's gonna dunk!* I was thinking.

As we were leaving the park an Air Force sergeant came walking up with his two toddlers, a three-year-old boy and a two-year-old girl. The dad was young and looked pretty sharp in his crisp uniform shirt, flight cap, and dark sunglasses. The boy trotted out in front chasing a tennis ball, and the girl carried a Barbie doll by the hair. The sergeant shot us a winning smile.

"Oh, back-a-ball!" the boy said, pointing at us.

"Do you want to try?" I asked. I held the basketball out to him and he quickly thumped over to his father and handed him the tennis ball. Then he came and took the basketball from me. "Dank you!" he said and began bouncing it. He could actually dribble pretty well for a kid his age.

"Wow, he's amazing!" I said.

The sergeant beamed. "It's all sports, sports, sports with this kid. His mom and I can barely keep up. She's across the road registering for a course right now, and Benny here couldn't let us pass up a playground."

The daughter was really shy. Her nose was smooshed against her father's leg the entire time he was talking.

"Go, Benny!" I called out as the little guy ran to the post and launched the ball about halfway up to the hoop. "We need to recruit this kid," I said and turned to Aggie. I noticed a darkness in her eyes that really surprised me. Her lips were pursed too, like she was fed up.

"What's wrong?" I said.

"Nothing," she said unconvincingly. "We need to get going." Then she turned to the sergeant. "Can we get our ball back?"

"Oh, sure," he said. "Benny! Come on, champ, these kids need to go home. I'll toss the tennis ball around with you."

"One more back-a-ball!" Benny said and took another shot halfway to the rim. He raised his hands in the air as though he had just nailed a game-winning three. Then he dribbled the ball back to us, losing control just a couple of times. Aggie snatched the ball mid-dribble and tucked it under her arm. She began crossing the street without even waiting for me.

"Hey, thanks," the sergeant said to me.

"No problem," I said. I pointed at Aggie's back and shrugged. He smiled and shrugged in response, as if to say, "Girls. Whatcha gonna do?"

"Bye, Benny," I said and gave him a high-five. "Keep practicing. Bye, girl with Barbie." She squeezed her father's leg so tight I was afraid she'd cut off his circulation.

"Boy, that was a little harsh," I announced when I caught up to Aggie. "What the heck was that all about?" She just kept walking. "Hey, what's your problem?" I asked and pulled her arm. The basketball bounced to the sidewalk and rolled onto the quadrangle.

I was totally unprepared to see tears rolling down Aggie's cheeks. I didn't know what was going on. "Hey," was all I could say, quietly. I instinctively took her in my arms. She tensed up for a moment, but then leaned in and rested her head on my shoulder. I patted her back while she sniffled. "It's okay," I said. I felt confused and sorry for Aggie, but at the same time I felt good that I could be there for her. We held on to each other in the noontime sun, still hot and sweaty from our game.

Aggie finally led me into the coolness of the tunnel connecting the library and Squires Hall. It was well-lit and pleasant smelling in there, a big improvement over the tunnel junction leading to the capsule at Foxtrot-Zero. I figured the UND tunnel must be bustling during the winter, but on this summer's day it was completely abandoned except for us. We sat on the floor, facing each other.

"My dad is a sergeant in the Air Force," Aggie said after a long silence.

"Oh," I said. I wanted to hear more if she was willing to tell more, but I didn't pry.

"He left my mom . . . He left all of us when Alex and I were only three. He met somebody else when he went for training at another base. I don't remember much about him, except that he used to take us to that same playground at University Park. It's probably the first place I ever dribbled a basketball. And now, for all I know, he's over in the Middle East or something."

"I'm really sorry," I said. "You never hear from him?"

She shook her head. "Never. My mom even quit taking support checks from him by the time Alex and I were six.

She said that since he stole our happiness as a family, accepting money from him would be like accepting it from a thief."

"That's a lousy situation, Aggie," I said. "I'm so sorry you have to deal with it."

She shrugged and gave me a forced smile.

"But you know who I feel sorry for more than anyone else?" I continued. "Your father. He's missing out on a lot. Anybody would be really proud of you and Alex. And personally, I would say especially *you*."

She actually smiled for real now. "You know something?" she said. "I think you're gonna be a social worker or a psychologist one of these days. Thank you for making me feel better." She leaned over and gave me a quick peck on the cheek before trotting off toward the Squires Hall end of the tunnel.

Looking at Aggie—athletic, funny, sensitive, and I would even say pretty in her own way—I realized that there would be no contest now on which girl I would want to share a blanket with at a fireworks show. And if Sarah Beasley happened to be there with her date—maybe even my old buddy Brandon—Aggie and I would toss them a friendly wave.

*You know what?* I was thinking. *Maybe I will become a social worker or psychologist someday.* I felt my cheek. *The pay's good.*

\*\*\*\*\*\*\*

After lunch, the four of us twins set up for a phone call in the Burkes' living room while Ms. Burke was off painting a lounge. This time we had voted for Mandy to make the call. She wasn't thrilled about it, but she was suddenly up to the challenge when I said, "Does bruh-boo need to do it again?" According to our parents, Mandy called me bruh-boo during our first year of talking. She hates being reminded of that.

Aggie dialed the number for Frank Henderson before activating the speakerphone and tape recorder. Mandy nervously cleared her throat and then looked relieved when only voicemail picked up. At the end of Mr. Henderson's greeting, he said, "If you're inquiring about buying or selling a home, you can reach me at Henderson Realty on North Forty-Second Street," and he gave another phone number. Aggie quickly wrote it down.

"Hey, Mandy's getting off too easy," I protested. She flashed a sickeningly sweet smile in response.

"Why don't we drop in on Frank Henderson?" Alex suggested. "North Forty-Second is just down the road."

"But Mandy's still taking the lead on this one," I said. "What's fair is fair," I added, borrowing an expression that our father often uses.

"Whatever you say, Daddy," Mandy responded.

*******

Mr. Henderson was the only person in the small, twin-desk realty office. One nameplate read FRANK HENDERSON and the other MARY ODEGARD. Mr. Henderson sat at his desk talking on the phone when we arrived. He was about seventy years old and had the longest comb-over I had ever seen. A comb-over is when a guy who's totally bald on top grows his side hair long enough to cover his baldness and reach the other side of his head. My mom considers a comb-over to be a kind of mortal sin. "George," she tells my father, "if you ever go bald, then just be bald for goodness' sake!" Mr. Henderson's comb-over was so long that it covered his ear on the other side. He held up a finger to indicate that he would be just one more minute.

"Now, what can I do for you kids?" he asked in a friendly voice when he got off the phone. Aggie reached into her denim purse and I knew she was clicking the

Record button. "Can I interest you in a nice split-level that's walking distance from the golf course? She's a real honey!" He laughed heartily, like that was a great joke or something.

We all laughed politely. "No sir," Mandy began, and I was glad to see that she was still up to the challenge. She opened the Red River High School yearbook to the dedication page and held it toward Mr. Henderson. "We're working on a special memorial project for Bobby Swenson, and we're just talking to people who may have known him."

Mr. Henderson's expression turned serious at the sound of Bobby's name. "Is that so?" he said. "Well, I didn't really know him well because he was a few years younger than me. Terrible thing about the way he died, though. My father had nightmares about that for years."

"Your father?" Mandy asked innocently. *That's right, sister—keep him talking!*

"Yes, my father was a construction worker on the site."

"And he was there the day Bobby died?" Mandy prodded.

"Yes, yes he was," Mr. Henderson said sadly. "In my father's nightmares, it was always *me* who fell in the pit. See, I had been working at that site too until Robert, Bobby's dad, set me straight. I was just a nineteen-year-old punk and I already had a problem with drinking. Robert took me aside and said that for my own safety and the safety of the rest of his crew, he couldn't afford to have me onsite anymore. He gave me the number for a counselor and told me to reapply when I got cleaned up."

"How did you feel about that?" Aggie asked.

"Mad. Really mad at first, and I blamed Robert for treating me unfairly. But after Bobby died, I got to thinking that could've been me. I could have easily stumbled into the pit myself. Kind of put things in perspective, if you know what I mean."

"So what happened?" Mandy asked.

"Well, I took Robert's advice and saw the counselor. I've been a teetotaler now since February, 1965. You know what that means? Not a drop of alcohol."

"Was your father upset with Mr. Swenson for firing you?" I asked. I was hoping he would say something like, "Between us, yes. My father hated that man so much I think he would have done anything to get revenge." I would have looked over at Aggie and given a knowing nod because she would have recorded that confession. However, that wasn't even close to Mr. Henderson's reply.

"Goodness no!" Mr. Henderson declared. "In fact, Dad was the one who tipped him off about my drinking in the first place. Dad credited Robert with saving my life . . . in more ways than one. First of all, I didn't get killed onsite. Plus, I wound up going to college. I got married, had kids, and started a pretty successful business for myself. Not bad, all in all."

"Wow!" I exclaimed. It wasn't a response to Mr. Henderson's success story, though; it was a response to the fact that we had once again slammed into a dead end in our search for Bobby's murderer.

"Well, that's my personal history," Mr. Henderson chuckled. "Sorry I can't help with more information on Bobby, though."

"That's okay," Alex said without enthusiasm.

"Hey, now . . . how much do you suppose that memorial will cost?" Mr. Henderson asked.

"We're not sure yet," Mandy responded. "But we're thinking about a bronze plaque on a wooden post."

"Well, whatever it costs, just have your parents send me the bill." He handed us a business card. "It's the least I can do to honor the son of the man who saved my life."

"Thank you so much," Mandy said graciously and accepted the card.

"Thank you," we all repeated and left the office. We stood on North Forty-Second Street in a daze. Were our sleuthing days over? Bobby would be so disappointed to hear that our leads had completely dried up and we were left with nothing now. I felt it should be my job to deliver the bad news to Bobby because of the more personal connection I had formed with him.

As we started to walk away, Mr. Henderson popped out of his office. "Hey kids, I've got an idea!" he called out enthusiastically. "Joe Blanchard will be in town for a fundraiser tomorrow evening. After all I've contributed to his campaign, I'm sure I can convince him to chat with you for a while. You know who he is, don't you?"

We all nodded our heads. "Congressman, running for U.S. Senate," Alex said.

"Right," Mr. Henderson said. "Well, you might be surprised to know that he was also one of Bobby's friends. Let me see that yearbook again."

Mr. Henderson opened to the "B" section of the junior class and found Joe Blanchard right away. He looked completely different from the way he appeared now in campaign ads. His dark hair was disheveled, he wore black-rimmed glasses, and he was quite overweight. It's like his face just barely fit into the width of the photo. The only extracurricular activity listed for him was "AV Club."

"What was the AV Club?" Mandy asked.

"Audio-Visual," Mr. Henderson said. "That means he got filmstrips ready and set up the PA system for school assemblies—things like that. Plus, he sometimes showed movies in the auditorium during lunch."

"And Bobby was good friends with him?" Alex asked.

"Well, in a way," Mr. Henderson said. "They grew up together on the same street and everything. Bobby actually got into a few fights when older guys were picking on Joe. Mean kids used to call him 'Roly-Poly Joey' back then. He had a hard time standing up for himself."

"Wow, that's a pretty amazing turnaround for Mr. Blanchard," I observed. "He went from *that* to becoming a U.S. congressman?"

"That's right," Mr. Henderson said. "After Bobby died, it was like Joey took it upon himself to fulfill Bobby's dreams. On the outside Bobby tried to keep up the rebel image, but people who knew him well say he had definite goals in life. He wanted to become a lawyer and then run for office of some kind."

"So you think Bobby's death inspired his friend to make something of himself?" Mandy asked.

"I would say so," Mr. Henderson reasoned. "The accident really shook him up, especially since he happened to show up at the site right after Bobby fell."

"He was there?" I asked excitedly. "Mr. Blanchard was at Foxtrot-Zero that day?" I couldn't believe that a new lead had just opened up for us.

"Yeah, strange coincidence," Mr. Henderson said. "Joey was dropping off something to his uncle, another one of the construction workers. When he found out what had just happened to his friend, Joey apparently passed out on the spot. That must've been a real eye-opener about just how fragile life can be."

We all nodded, not knowing what to say. *This is big*, I was thinking. *Maybe even huge!*

"Well, anyway," Mr. Henderson continued, "Joey should be able to provide you with any extra information you need about Bobby. Tomorrow after 6:00 PM, call the cell number on that card I gave you. I'll tell you what the plan is. Okay?"

"Okay, great!" we exclaimed. I'm sure we all wanted to find out more about the "strange coincidence" of Joey Blanchard showing up at Foxtrot-Zero at about the same time as Bobby's fall. That sounded very suspicious.

"Only don't get me into trouble by calling him Joey, or Roly-Poly Joey, for that matter," Mr. Henderson laughed. "Mr. Blanchard or Congressman would be more appropriate."

"Okay, thanks again," Mandy said happily.

Just then, a breeze sneaked up on poor Mr. Henderson and shot his comb-over nine inches straight up in the air. He looked crazed and we all laughed; we couldn't help it. Fortunately, Mr. Henderson was a good sport about it. "Whoa, I definitely hate when *that* happens!" he said and laughed along with us. He smoothed down his hair and retreated to the safety of his office.

# CHAPTER THIRTEEN

The next day was Friday, and all we could do was hold on until 6:00 PM. My mom had only a morning class that day, so we convinced her to let us spend the afternoon and night at the Burkes' apartment. I would camp out on Alex's bedroom floor, and Mandy would do the same in Aggie's room.

"Absolutely, they are more than welcome!" Ms. Burke said happily when Mom dropped us off at the apartment. Ms. Burke seemed proud to be taking a turn for a sleepover. "We'll have a good time."

"I'll go ahead and surprise George then," Mom said. She was all smiles. "We'll head out to dinner in East Grand, catch a late movie, and then spend the night in a hotel."

"Excellent idea," Ms. Burke said. "And get a room with a Jacuzzi." The two moms giggled.

To make the time pass a little faster until 6:00, we twins took a long walk to Red River High School to return the yearbook. It was a pretty hot day—at least eighty degrees—but the humidity was low for a change and there were lots of gusty breezes.

"Hey, check me out!" I demanded during one of the gusts. I put my hand on top of my head and made my fingers flail around as though they were hairs. Everyone laughed and I felt a little guilty for making fun of Mr.

Henderson. "He is such a nice guy," I added to ease my conscience. Everyone nodded in agreement.

"Hi, Mrs. Hyslop," Mandy and Alex said when we entered the high school office. Mrs. Hyslop was the same secretary they had talked to before. Her red hair was pulled into a tight bun on top of her head and she wore black, cat-rimmed glasses. She had what my parents would call a "zany look" about her.

"Hello, you two," Mrs. Hyslop replied happily. "It looks like you're multiplying. Who are your friends?"

As Mandy explained the situation, Alex walked over to a bookcase and returned the yearbook to its proper slot. He then pulled out the next yearbook and began flipping through its pages. *What's he looking for?* I wondered. Whatever it was, he had found it. Alex suddenly looked over at me with that *Aha!* look in his eyes. He snapped the book shut and said, "Mrs. Hyslop, do you mind if we borrow this yearbook for a day or two—the one from the 1965-1966 school year?"

"Be my guest," she said. "I don't think it'll help you with your project, though. That was our senior year and, as you know, Bobby was already gone."

"I thought Mr. Blanchard might like to see it," Alex said. "He'll be in town today and there's a good chance we'll get to talk to him."

Mrs. Hyslop looked confused about why a national politician would be interested in talking to four kids. Aggie explained that Mr. Henderson was setting up the meeting for us.

"Hey, lucky you!" Mrs. Hyslop said. "I can't afford to donate the kind of money you need to attend Joe's fundraiser. But tell him I said hello and that he has my vote, okay? I voted for him for senior class president and I've been voting for him ever since."

"Did he win the class president election?" I asked.

"By a landslide," she said. "Just about every student in the class voted for him because we all knew he was doing it for Bobby. In a way, it was as though Joe had *become* Bobby. I mean, look at the drastic change in him in just one year."

Mrs. Hyslop retrieved the yearbook Alex had just returned and set it on a counter along with the newer yearbook. She opened them side-by-side to the pages that showed Joe Blanchard's pictures. On the left was the bespectacled, roly-poly king of the AV Club. On the right was the thinned-out Senior Class President who had lost his glasses and apparently gained a lot of confidence. You could see that new confidence in his restless smile and the way he now wore his hair, swept back like . . . James Dean. Like Bobby. I'm not sure, but he may have even lightened his hair!

"Contact lenses were kind of a newfangled invention back then," Mrs. Hyslop said. "But see what a difference a set of contacts and a new attitude can make? Of course, I'm still partial to my own glasses because I think they capture my personality."

Mrs. Hyslop made two sideways peace signs in front of her glasses, and then slid her fingers to either side of her head. She even shimmied down toward the floor while doing that, and we all laughed as we left the school office. My initial impression of Mrs. Hyslop had been correct: Zany!

"You know, it's too weird how much Mr. Blanchard changed in one year," I announced to my fellow twins when we were outside. "There's something really suspicious about his connection to Bobby."

"And you don't even know the whole story yet," Alex said in the tone of someone who's guarding a juicy secret. "Not even close."

"What else do you know?" Aggie asked and playfully raised a fist. "I haven't given you a good pounding in a while, so don't give me an excuse now."

"Okay, okay," Alex said. He stopped walking, and the rest of us did as well. Alex flipped through the yearbook and then casually pointed at a picture. He didn't say anything. He didn't have to because the picture told the whole story: There was Joe Blanchard—all smiles—at the Christmas Ball, and his date was none other than Jennifer Franklin.

"Oh *man!*" we all gasped. Of course, I had already told Mandy and the Burke twins about Bobby's feelings for Jennifer. I didn't think Bobby would mind, and I figured the others had a right to know as much about the case as I did. So the picture of Blanchard with Jennifer hit each of us like a karate chop to the back of the neck.

And then Alex quietly flipped to another page and pointed. This picture delivered a savage kick to my gut: There they were again, Joe and Jennifer, only this time as king and queen of the Senior Prom.

"See his hand on Jennifer's back?" Alex asked, touching the picture. "I think it was on someone else's the year before."

Just for a moment I could swear I felt the impression of a hand on my back. I shuddered. "I'll bet he snuck up behind Bobby without anyone noticing him," I said in a daze. "He wanted Jennifer. He did it because he wanted the girl."

"And the popularity," Aggie said.

"And the power," Mandy added.

Alex nodded in agreement with us. We all just stood there in a tense silence under the spell of our discovery. "Now that we're all on the same page," Alex finally said, "we need to discover if we're right."

We went back to the Burkes' apartment hoping that Mr. Henderson would come through for us. Was Mr. Blanchard capable of murder? Or at least *had* he been capable of committing such a horrifying act when he was a teenager? We had to find out for ourselves. It would have been great to get Bobby's advice on the situation before our meeting with Mr. Blanchard, but that was impossible because we had no way to get back to Foxtrot-Zero. Ms. Burke's car was in the shop for repair, and even if it wasn't, we wouldn't have had the nerve to ask her to drive eighty minutes roundtrip.

We killed some time playing hide-and-seek in the UND tunnels and tossing around a Frisbee on the quadrangle outside Squires Hall. There were so few students living on campus during the summer that we had the whole area to ourselves. Late in the afternoon, Mandy and Alex sat under a tree and read aloud a mystery while Aggie and I did a little lawn bowling. I loved the *clunk* sound that the bocce balls made when they knocked together, but it was hard to stay focused on anything other than our mission.

And then, finally . . . six o'clock! The four of us were huddled around the Burkes' phone at the exact moment the second hand joined the minute hand at the top of the hour. Ms. Burke was in the kitchen, but that didn't stop us. We had already told her our cover story about dedicating a memorial in Bobby's honor, so she wasn't suspicious when we mentioned our chance to meet with Joe Blanchard.

"Hello, Mr. Henderson? It's Aggie Burke calling about-"

"Well, you kids are in luck!" Mr. Henderson said over the speakerphone before Aggie could go any further. We could hear muffled conversations and laughter in the background. "Our congressman here is on a tight schedule, but he loves kids and said that he could meet with you for a little while."

"Oh, that's terrific!" Aggie exclaimed. We all gave her the thumbs-up.

"It'll be a little late, though," Mr. Henderson said apologetically. "We'll see you in front of the Chester Fritz Library at nine o'clock. Okay? I'll be along for the ride as well."

"We'll be there," Aggie said. "Thank you so much."

Ms. Burke walked into the living room at the end of the conversation. We convinced her to allow us to go, but only after she'd conferred with my parents on their cell phone. Mom and Dad thought it was a unique opportunity to meet with a congressman, so they agreed to the plan.

*******

It was still pretty light outside at 9:00 PM. In fact, if Aggie and I had time we could have gone over to the park and shot a game of one-on-one without needing any artificial lighting at all. My dad had told me that summer days are so long in Grand Forks because of how far north it is.

A long, black limousine—a stretch limo—rolled up to the curb a few minutes after 9:00. The tinted rear window eased down far enough for us to see the friendly smile of Mr. Henderson. "Hi, kids!" he said. He was watching TV right there in the car.

"*Murder, She Wrote!*" Mandy exclaimed. Sure enough, there was the old mystery-solver, Jessica, questioning some well-dressed man in an art museum. We twins looked at each other in amazement; of all the things Mr. Henderson could have been watching, what were the odds that it would be an episode of *Murder, She Wrote*?

"Yeah, my wife and I love this show," Mr. Henderson said.

A chauffeur got out of the limo and opened the other back door. Mr. Blanchard hopped out and walked around to where we were gathered. He was wearing a white shirt and black bowtie, but his tuxedo jacket was slung casually over his shoulder. It was weird to have him there in person after seeing his face only on billboards and on TV. Like a wax museum figure that had suddenly come to life, Mr. Blanchard flashed a dazzling smile and shook each of our hands. *Is this the hand of a murderer?* I wondered as he shook mine.

"So, Frank tells me you kids want to honor the memory of an old friend of mine," he said enthusiastically. "Well, I think that's very noble of you."

"How about on the steps?" the chauffeur said, motioning toward the library with a camera.

"This is what they call a photo-op, kids," Mr. Blanchard said. "Bear with me for a moment here."

We followed him to the library steps, and the chauffeur arranged us so that Aggie and I were seated on one side of Mr. Blanchard and Mandy and Alex on the other. "Look at *him*, not at *me!*" the crabby chauffeur ordered, and we did as we were told. *Click, click, click.*

The chauffeur trotted to the driver's side of the limo and opened the same door that Mr. Blanchard had exited. The chauffeur raised his right hand and pointed dramatically at his watch on the other wrist.

"Well, kids, what can I tell you?" Mr. Blanchard began, ignoring the driver. There was one more *click*, and I knew that Aggie had started recording. "Bobby Swenson was a good friend," Mr. Blanchard continued. "He was one of those rare people who's the whole package, an all-arounder if you know what I mean. Pretty much successful at everything in life."

"Let's go, sir," the chauffeur called out.

"Sorry, but it looks like that's all the time I have," Mr. Blanchard said to us and stood up. "One more gathering tonight and then back to Washington in the morning. So, best of luck to you all. Oh, and remind your parents to vote in November!"

We all sat there, stunned, as Mr. Blanchard walked down the steps. *That was it? That was the meeting we had pinned all our hopes on?* I couldn't take it. I thought about poor Bobby being left alone at Foxtrot-Zero—just like that baby had been left alone in his car seat—and that gave me the courage to step forward.

"Congressman!" I blurted out and trotted down the steps. Mr. Blanchard stopped and turned. My heart was racing like crazy and I had to steady my breathing before I continued. "Can I ask you a personal question?"

"Sure, anything," he responded good-naturedly.

I motioned for him to lean in toward me. "Why did you push him?" I whispered so no one else could hear.

Mr. Blanchard froze on the spot and his face went absolutely white. "What did you say?" he laughed nervously.

I got even closer to his ear this time and said through my teeth, the way my father does when he's exasperated, "Why . . . did . . . you . . . push . . . Bobby?"

"Sir, let's go!" the chauffeur demanded.

"Just a minute," Mr. Blanchard shot back. He was clearly agitated now; I saw the caged animal look in his eyes. He put a hand on my shoulder and leaned in threateningly.

"We have proof at Foxtrot-Zero," I said.

"Listen, boy, I have no idea what you're talking about, but you're giving me the creeps," he hissed. I could smell whisky on his breath. "So just shut your g-- d--- mouth, got it?" He actually swore at me!

"No problem," I said. My heart was thumping so hard I could feel it in my throat, but I managed to keep up a tough guy act. "I'll keep it shut right up until I talk to a reporter at the *Herald*."

"We're gonna be late!" the chauffeur complained. He even reached into the limo and beeped the horn.

"Shut up!" Mr. Blanchard barked. Then he squeezed my shoulder so hard that it hurt. He was strong and appeared much younger than a guy in his late sixties. "Don't play with fire," he whispered. "You know what happens when you do that, right? You get burned. All of you get burned."

Then he straightened up and put on that fake smile again as though nothing unpleasant had just taken place. "Have a great night, kids," he said happily. "It was a pleasure to meet all of you."

As Mr. Blanchard trotted over to his impatient chauffeur, I walked up to Mr. Henderson's open window and shook his hand. On the little TV screen, Jessica sat rigidly with a piece of duct tape over her mouth while the well-dressed man pointed a gun at her.

"Did you kids find out what you needed?" Mr. Henderson asked.

"Yes," I said. "Definitely."

# CHAPTER FOURTEEN

It was one o'clock in the morning and none of us could sleep. Naturally, the other twins had freaked out when I told them about my conversation with Mr. Blanchard. And now we were clustered on Alex's bedroom floor considering our next step. We still wanted to get Bobby's advice, and we even tried a kind of séance to see if we could coax him to Alex's room. No such luck.

My talk about going to *The Grand Forks Herald* had been a bluff, of course. We couldn't very well accuse a U.S. congressman of a fifty-year-old murder based on just our hunch and a few whisky-stinking words. Our situation was urgent now because we wanted to see what kind of guidance Bobby could give us before Mr. Blanchard headed back to Washington, D.C. So, that's when I came up with the crazy idea of going to Foxtrot-Zero right away.

We knew that no buses were running at that time of night, so we brainstormed every other way to get there while Aggie jotted them down in her spiral notebook. One by one we eliminated modes of transportation that were either too impractical, like riding bikes, or too dangerous, like hitchhiking. We considered calling Mr. Henderson and explaining the whole situation to him, but chances were he wouldn't believe us. The one idea that Aggie had left on the page was *Taxi*. She circled it.

Alex looked up a local taxi service online and dialed the number. Alex made his voice deep and asked how much it would cost to get a ride from UND out to Foxtrot-Zero. Apparently the taxi dispatcher didn't have a clue where Foxtrot-Zero was because Alex had to give directions in detail.

"That much, huh?" Alex said. "Well, okay then. We'll be waiting out in front of the Chester Fritz Library in fifteen minutes."

"Fifty-five dollars," Alex announced when he hung up the phone.

"Fifty-five dollars?" Aggie repeated. "Are you nuts? I know it's a long ride, but that's all the money we have between the two of us."

"We'll pay you back our share when we get there," Mandy said.

Aggie quickly wrote a note and tore it out of her spiral:

*Good morning, Mom! We decided to get moving early today. I have the cell phone with me, so call us if you need to.*
*Love,*
*Aggie*

Aggie left the note on the kitchen counter and put the cell phone in her denim purse. Alex picked up the yearbook, and we all tiptoed out of the apartment. The note was a very good idea, I thought. Assuming, of course, that Ms. Burke didn't wake up anytime soon and find it.

It was chilly outside, with a light mist in the air. And I don't care how far north we were, it was also very dark now, especially since clouds were blotting out the moonglow. We walked over to the library concocting an elaborate story to feed to the taxi driver. We would tell him that we were sleeping over a friend's house near campus, and the fire alarm kept going off for no reason and waking everybody up. The friend's parents finally decided that we should just head home and get some sleep.

As it turned out we didn't need the story at all. "You're going out to Baxter's place, right?" the cab driver asked casually when we got in. He was around fifty years old and had a stubbly beard. I didn't recognize the expression "Baxter's place" at first because I hadn't thought about Foxtrot-Zero's owner in a long time. I thought of the site as Bobby's place, not Tommy Baxter's. "Yes, that's right," I finally said from the back seat. "Foxtrot-Zero."

And that was the extent of our conversation during the forty-minute ride. The radio was tuned softly to an oldies station and I think each of us twins slept for a while during the trip. I know *I* did, even though I was so excited to hear what Bobby had to say. I woke up at one point and found Aggie asleep on my shoulder. I smiled and dozed off again while breathing in the sweet, cozy smell of her hair. With the straight road, the gently glowing dashboard lights, the soft music, and the soothing *swish* of the windshield wipers, I'm surprised that the driver didn't fall asleep as well.

Finally, the cab pulled up the access road to Foxtrot-Zero and stopped just in front of the gate. One light, which my parents had set up on a timer, was glowing inside the house. An outdoor security light was also on, but it didn't help much. The eerie lighting reminded me of my father's favorite description in literature, written centuries ago by a poet named John Milton. Milton described fire in hell as not giving light, but instead just making darkness visible. That's the impression I got after the cab pulled away and we stood under the security light—before the gate of Foxtrot-Zero—on that moonless, dreary night.

Thunder rumbled lazily in the distance and moaned its way across the sky, toward us. I crouched down and fumbled with a few stones to find the fake, hollow one where my parents hid a spare gate key. Headlights suddenly crept toward us on the access road.

"Did we leave anything in the cab?" Mandy asked.

"No," Alex said. "I've got the yearbook right here."

The car's high-beams suddenly kicked on and moved toward us fast. We all stood shielding our eyes from the glare. I had found the key by now and it was dangling from my fingertips on a keyring.

"Jeez, is this guy trying to blind us, or what?" I complained and froze like an escaping prisoner caught in the beam of a searchlight.

When the car came to a halt we saw that it wasn't the cab at all; it was a Cadillac. The engine stopped and the headlights went out, leaving only the dull glow of parking lights. The door opened and out came . . . Joe Blanchard.

"Oh my God!" we all yelled.

"Hiya, kids!" he called out sarcastically.

A bolt of lightning flashed nearby, illuminating our creepy scene for a long moment. I wished another bolt would strike Blanchard and drop him in his tracks. *Can Bobby make that happen?* I wondered.

Blanchard stuck a long flashlight under his chin and began walking toward us. "Surprised to see me?" he asked. Whenever Dad does that with a flashlight I think it's just goofy. Seeing Blanchard do it, though, made me sick.

I tried frantically to insert the key into the lock. "Come on, come on!" the twins were saying, but my hands were shaking so much that I dropped the key. I reached down but couldn't find it. Instead, I picked up a stone the size of my palm. Without warning I turned and launched it with all my might at Blanchard. I heard the thud and figured that I hit him in the arm because the flashlight suddenly dropped to the ground.

"Ow, you little—" I heard him say.

"Run!" I commanded. My guess was that Blanchard had some kind of weapon, so we couldn't take a chance on rushing him.

The four of us dashed deep into the sunflower fields. I ran so hard that I got a metallic, bloody taste in my mouth even though I knew I wasn't bleeding. In the panic and darkness we twins got separated, and I suddenly realized I was all alone. I was dying to know where the others were, but I didn't call out because that would have given away my position. I crouched down among the sunflower stalks and looked back toward Foxtrot-Zero through the mist. The faint, distant glow of the security light told me just how far I had run. So many questions tumbled and pinged through my mind: *How could this be happening? Where are the others? Will my parents come charging up the access road and pull us out of this nightmare? Can't Bobby do something to help us?*

And then I saw a light bobbing through the field about fifty yards from me. I knew it was Blanchard searching with his flashlight, so I stayed low and did the best I could to control my breathing and stay calm. *Everything's gonna work out. Everything will be fine.* The ground was cold and damp, and the smell of rich soil was so strong that it mingled with the taste of blood in my mouth. I thought I might vomit.

"No, let go of me!" I heard Aggie scream.

"Leave her alone!" Alex yelled, and then he called out in a terrified voice, "Mark!"

*Stay still,* my inner voice told me. *Or get up and run; there's no way this old man could catch you.* And then my mind jumped back to the day when Brandon and I were being chased— the day when I earned that horrible nickname, Ten-Point-Eight. Brandon had called out to me the same way: "Mark!" I knew he called, and I knew from the sound of his panicked cry that he had fallen to the ground. I convinced myself that I didn't hear anything and kept running.

Reggie Williams and his father had seen the older boys beating Aaron and ran outside to break it up. By the time I made it back to the scene, Mr. Williams was carrying Brandon into his house. He had a swollen face and a cracked rib, and I've never been able to forgive myself for that. "Brandon!" I cried. His mouth was bleeding and his face looked terrible. "I didn't know you fell!" I said. "I didn't know!" Tears streamed down my face.

Lying now in the sunflower field, I felt as though Brandon's eyes were staring down at me from his bruised face. I had to do something. "No!" I yelled and jumped to my feet. "Blanchard, get away from them!" I stood there shaking, and the flashlight suddenly pointed directly at my face.

"Game's over, kids," Blanchard yelled. "Ollie-ollie oxen free! Now, everybody moves back to the gate with me before anything bad happens here."

"Mark?" I heard Mandy cry out. She sounded terrified. Blanchard shined the light on her about twenty feet away. I ran over and hugged my sister, and then we joined the other twins and walked back toward Foxtrot-Zero in a daze. A lightning flash revealed that Blanchard was wearing rubber gloves and that one of them was planted on Mandy's shoulder.

"Just get your hand off her," I said. "We're not going anywhere."

"Okay, tough guy. Don't wind up being a dumb guy too," Blanchard hissed and gave Mandy a push forward. She stumbled, but didn't fall. "Nobody gets hurt if you all follow directions." His words floated in a mist of whiskey.

Blanchard used his flashlight at the gate to search for the key. What he found first was the yearbook, which Alex had dropped before running. "Hey, now that was a good year," Blanchard said and brushed raindrops from the cover. "I always tell people that's when my career in politics really got started."

"Yeah, after getting Bobby out of the way first," I added.

"There you go again," Blanchard chuckled and then threw the yearbook so hard against my stomach that it took my breath away. I doubled over in pain. "Now we're even," he said.

"You jerk!" Mandy yelled and put a hand on my back. "What did you have to do that for?"

"What did he have to throw a stone at me for?" Blanchard shot back, mocking Mandy. He finally found the key and unlocked the gate. "Oh, and my arm is feeling fine now, by the way. In case any of you were worried."

"Our parents will wake up as soon as we go in," Mandy warned. "And you don't want to mess with our dad."

"How stupid do you think I am?" Blanchard snickered. "I was casing this place for more than two hours and I know no one's home. Having you kids show up on your own in the middle of the night was a most pleasant surprise. So, I suppose I should thank you all for displaying such incredible stupidity. Thanks!"

I hated Blanchard more than ever for toying with us like that. He rolled the gate shut behind us and directed us toward the house. The misty drizzle opened up into a major downpour as we entered. Blanchard turned on the light in the recreation room and made the four of us sit on the pool table so he could keep an eye on us. He sure didn't look like the tuxedoed man we had met on the steps of the Chester Fritz. He was now wearing a black stocking cap, an old pair of blue jeans, a hooded sweatshirt with a rip at the elbow, and a pair of raggedy Converse basketball shoes.

"Pretend the floor is a pool of acid and the tabletop is your safety zone," he advised. "Do kids still play games like that?"

We all kept our mouths shut. I had my breath back by now, but I wasn't about to waste it on him. I focused on the sound of the rain slapping its way across the roof in sheets. *Come on, Bobby. Zap this guy right through the window.*

"See, I believe in being open and honest with people, so let me tell you what's going on here. For one thing, you should know that I'm a very careful man. No fingerprints or hairs left behind." Blanchard held out his gloved hands and flailed his fingers for a moment, and then pointed to his stocking cap. "And I even trash-picked these clothes so I can just throw them away again after our . . . meeting here tonight. That way if anything unpleasant happens, it won't come back to haunt me."

Then the worst thing that I could ever imagine happened: Blanchard reached into his sweatshirt pocket and pulled out a gun. "No!" we all yelled. We locked our arms around each other and started crying. Who knew what this man was capable of doing to us?

"Oh, dry your eyes," Blanchard said in disgust. "This is all perfectly legal. I have a permit to conceal and carry this weapon anywhere I choose. Now, here's the thing. I can't afford to have people going around calling me a murderer while I'm trying to become a United States Senator. You see my predicament?"

Again, we said nothing; we were all too scared.

"Okay, you said you have proof that I pushed Bobby to his death," Blanchard continued. "I know that's impossible since I didn't do it. But like I said, I'm a careful man. I make sure all my T's are crossed and all my I's are dotted. So, once we straighten out this *proof* thing, it'll be as though this night never even happened."

"The proof we're talking about is down in the launch control center," I managed to say. Anger was beginning to replace my fear, and I stopped crying. I had no idea what would happen in the capsule, but I had a hunch that Bobby would know how to handle the situation.

"Don't mess with me!" Blanchard shouted.

"He's not," Mandy replied, trying to sound brave. "We can show you."

"Okay, I'll play along," Blanchard said. "So now we all take a little underground fieldtrip."

The elevator ride seemed to take three times longer than usual. Nobody said anything on the way down, but we twins locked eyes with each other to boost our courage. None of us cried anymore because we were all either too numb or too angry by now. I kept my hands firmly in my pants pockets, though, to hide how shaky they were. I looked up at Blanchard's profile. *What will this man do if he doesn't like what he's about to discover in the capsule?* I wondered. As if he was reading my mind, Blanchard twisted his mouth into a half-smile and rested his hand on the gun, which he had returned to his sweatshirt pocket.

"Hello?" I called out as we entered the capsule, where the Beach Boys song "Be True to Your School" was playing quietly on the boombox. My confidence level shot higher within the familiar environment of the capsule. It felt like we twins had suddenly gained the home-field advantage that athletes hope for when facing their toughest rivals. Yes, the Foxtrot-Zero capsule was *our* turf, and we could only hope that Bobby would somehow be able to serve as our secret weapon.

"Hello," Bobby's computer voice said. And then after a pause, "Who is with you?"

Blanchard grabbed my arm and pulled me along to where the laptop computer was perched in front of the slifix. "Who's keying that in on the computer?" he demanded, looking at the screen.

I smiled wickedly at Blanchard. "Hey Bobby," I said, "we have a friend of yours with us."

"Bobby?" Blanchard mocked me. "What's that supposed to mean?"

"Why bring someone here without checking with me first?" Bobby asked. "I don't know this person."

"I'm sorry, Bobby," I said. "We can explain."

"We need your help, Bobby!" Mandy cried out.

"What are you—" Bobby began.

"Okay, now just shut up, everybody!" Blanchard interrupted. He shook his head and looked totally fed up. "I'm tired of playing your little game. What so-called proof down here are you talking about?"

"Joey Blanchard?" Bobby said. "Is that you?"

"What?" Blanchard said, staring at the laptop. "I want to know *who* is keying in these words. Tell me now."

"I know this is going to sound unbelievable," the computer responded to him, "but it's me, Bobby Swenson."

A moment of terror flashed across Blanchard's face. But then he suddenly had the look of a man setting down the last piece of a large jigsaw puzzle. "So, you're computer whiz kids, huh?" he said, glaring at each of us in turn. "Trying to make a fool out of me and get me to say something regrettable. Who put you up to this? Was it Demers' people?"

Richard Demers was the candidate running against him for senator. We all knew that from TV ads and billboards.

"No one put us up to anything," Mandy spoke up. "We just found Bobby down here and we're trying to help him figure something out."

"Bobby, right," Blanchard sneered. "You've got nothing here, kids. Just some computer-generated nonsense. You've wasted my time, and I don't have a lot of it."

"Do you still have your AV card, Joey?" Bobby asked. "Remember the time Steve and Roger switched film reels on you, and you started showing a girlie movie right there in the high school auditorium?"

Blanchard stared suspiciously at the computer. "How did you know about that?"

"Or the time you took a turn on Anita's brand new pogo stick," Bobby continued, "and broke the spring because . . . Well, for an obvious reason back then."

Bobby's Microsoft Sam voice had become less robotic and more conversational. Maybe having his old acquaintance in the capsule had somehow caused this change.

"Okay, that's it!" Blanchard roared. He looked frantically around the capsule. "Ollie-ollie oxen free!" he called out sarcastically.

"Still an unbeliever?" Bobby said. "Go ahead. You can ask me anything."

"*You* should be the one asking questions, Bobby," I jumped in. "Like why your friend Joey here pushed you in the pit back in 1964."

"What? Why would you say something like that?" Bobby asked.

"Here, look!" Alex said. He opened the yearbook to the picture of Joe Blanchard as senior class president.

"That's unexpected," Bobby said. "But it doesn't mean he pushed me. He wasn't even here that day."

"Yes, he *was* here," Mandy insisted. "He was at Foxtrot-Zero the day you died."

"There's more," Alex continued. He turned to the Christmas Ball picture of Joe and Jennifer. And then Alex flipped to the senior prom picture and held it in front of the slifix for a long time. There were Joe and Jennifer in all their youthful, royal splendor. "A Young Man Is Gone" started playing on the boombox, and I swear it seemed like the soundtrack for the real-life movie that was unfolding before our eyes.

"Why'd you do it?" Bobby asked quietly. Blanchard didn't say anything. "Look at me," Bobby said. And then again: "Look at me!" Only this time it was a human teenager's voice, and it came booming through the speakers on both the commander's and deputy's consoles. I was petrified and excited at the sound of Bobby's own voice, which had been silenced for the past fifty years. If he could suddenly talk the way he used to, what else would he be able to do? Blanchard was completely flustered. He pulled out his gun and actually pointed it at the computer.

"Look, it's *him*!" Aggie cried out, pointing at the slifix window. It was Bobby! There—in the slifix window—the photograph that Alex once fed into the computer had suddenly come to life. Now we twins really felt like we had the home-field advantage.

"Bobby!" the four of us yelled and actually jumped up and down. Blanchard's reaction was different. He crouched down and, with a stony expression, stared at the face of his old friend.

"I knew you my entire life and I could always tell when you were lying," Bobby said in the tone of a father scolding his child. When Bobby talked, you saw his lips moving in the slifix window, but you heard his voice through the console speakers. This separation between his face and his voice made an eerie situation seem even eerier. "Now look at me and tell me what happened that day."

"My God, Bobby?" Blanchard gasped and dropped to his knees in front of the slifix. The familiar voice—and the tone of that voice—must have convinced Blanchard that he was indeed face to face with his old friend. "Bobby, I swear to you—"

"Don't lie to me, Joey!" Bobby boomed.

"Okay, okay," Blanchard said quietly. "I never planned to do it, I swear to God. It was a crazy coincidence that I was out on the site the same time as you. I never planned-"

"But you did wind up doing it, didn't you?" Bobby asked. "Why?"

"Do you have any idea how hard it was to grow up on the same street with you?" Blanchard asked bitterly. "Just based on our looks alone, you were a winner and I was a loser. From the average person's point of view, at least. All the girls wanted to go out with you and all the boys wanted to *be* you. . . . And I was especially sick of my own parents always making comparisons: 'Bobby made the honor roll again, even with all the time he puts into football.' Or, as my father used to say, 'I keep hoping that kid will rub off on you one of these days.' Well, the old man finally got his wish, didn't he?"

Blanchard got up from his knees and sat down at the commander's console. He swiveled the chair to face the slifix and crossed his arms like a defiant defendant in a courtroom. He wanted to show Bobby and the rest of us that *he* was the one in charge now.

"You were a risk-taker, Bobby," Blanchard continued. "You got closer to the pit than you should have. No one noticed that because of all the commotion on site, and no one noticed me either. Without even thinking I felt my hand go to your back, and at that moment I became a risk-taker too. Poor old Roly-Poly Joey. An opportunity presented itself to me, and I took it." He added with a twisted laugh, "In a way, you should be proud of me."

"You're a sick man, Joe," Bobby said quietly. "I feel sorry for you."

"Don't you *ever* feel sorry for me," Blanchard shouted and thumped the speaker on the commander's console. "*I'm* the one who became class president. *I'm* the one who went to the ball and prom with Jennifer Franklin. And *I'm* the one who graduated from college and law school and became a national leader. I even received a Bobby Swenson Prelaw Scholarship at Minnesota State. Now there's a bit of irony for you!"

Blanchard stared at the slifix window and waited for a response from Bobby, but he didn't get one. None of us said anything. It made me sick to think of how much Blanchard had stolen from Bobby and his parents.

Blanchard continued. "So now you're telling me that a pathetic cartoon character stuck in a little window is gonna feel sorry for *me*? No, I don't think so, pal! I'm the one who got it all . . . everything you ever dreamed of."

"Did she marry you?" Bobby asked, sounding ill.

"Jennifer?" Blanchard scoffed. "She turned out not to be my type after all. Plus, she went and died a couple of years after high school."

"What?" Bobby raged. "Did you have anything to do with that?"

"Last time I checked I wasn't able to cause cancer. So I would have to say . . . um, no."

"I could have been there for her," Bobby said sadly. "Do you even care about how much pain you've caused?"

Blanchard stood up. "Okay, look. This session is over," he announced. "Where's the computer that runs this place?" he asked us twins. "And don't even try to mess with me. I've got a plane to catch."

Alex reluctantly pointed to the rack of equipment that contained the computer. Blanchard read the labels on the panels and then slid out the Memory Controller Group drawer. He took a hammer from a nearby tool chest and said, "Say bye-bye to your little friend."

"No!" we yelled.

The claw end of the hammer suddenly shot back at Blanchard, opening a gash above his right eyebrow. Blanchard swore at Bobby.

"Do it again, Bobby!" we yelled.

But it was too late; Blanchard struck the Memory Controller Group with all his might. He was a raging madman with blood dripping down his face.

"Don't you dare—" Bobby started to say.

*Bam!*

"hurt those"

*Bam-bam-bam!*

"kids!"

*Bam!*

The insides of the Memory Controller Group were mangled now, and the last thing we ever heard Bobby say was, "Don't you dare hurt those kids." Even as his link to the outside world was being hammered out of existence, Bobby could only think about our safety. Blanchard took out the gun and shot two bullets into the metal, just to make sure he had finished the job.

I ran over to the slifix, my ears ringing from the gunshots, and dropped down to window level. It was just clear glass now. "Bobby?" I said. I flipped the printer switch back to the On position, but nothing happened. "Bobby?" I felt tears running down my cheeks. I was so sad to lose our friend and so angry and frustrated about the whole situation. Anything could happen to us now. Blanchard was a total psycho, no doubt about it.

"Well, what we have here is definitely a problem," Blanchard said with his eyes narrowed in thought. He took a handkerchief out of his pocket and held it to his wound. A diagonal blood-streak on his face made him look like the devil. "You kids obviously know too much, but unfortunately you don't have little hard drives that I can neatly bash in. And, to be perfectly honest with you, I'm not fond of blood. Not mine or anyone else's for that matter."

"We won't say anything," I lied and wiped away my tears.

"No, of course you won't, cry baby," Blanchard said and pinched my cheek. "Remember what I told you about playing with fire? Well, now I'm afraid we're going to have a terrible accident upstairs. Let's go."

He held out his gun and motioned us toward the exit. Anger gurgled through my body, tensing my muscles and making my face red hot. I resolved that we had to do something. Four against one, and it was *our* turf; we couldn't just give in to this creep, this human devil. I pointed at my chest and made a little chopping motion, and then I pointed at the other twins and made a pushing motion. I kept my gestures small and in front of my body so that Blanchard, who was standing behind us, couldn't see them. I just hoped that my fellow twins were able to follow my plan. There was only one way to find out.

"Now!" I shouted as we entered the capsule's kitchenette. I wheeled around and chopped Blanchard's wrist. The gun dropped out of his hand, sliding over the edge of the suspended floor and clanking out of reach to the bottom of the capsule. The other twins triple-teamed him with a hard shove, slamming his back against the huge shock isolator. Instead of falling to the floor, though, his body started sliding up the isolator! Blanchard thrashed his arms around while he moved so far up that his knees were even with my forehead.

"Bobby, let me go!" he cried out in terror. "Come on, I was just trying to scare the kids."

"Call 911!" I yelled.

"There's no cell reception down here," Aggie reminded me. "Will the phone line work?"

"It's not connected to the computer," I said. "Go try it!"

While Aggie and Alex ran to the deputy's console, I grabbed two hammers from the toolbox and returned to where Blanchard was dangling. I gave one hammer to Mandy and held the other one up by my ear just in case Blanchard came back to floor level and we had to knock him out.

"You okay?" I asked my sister with a forced smile.

"I will be when this is all over," she replied with wide eyes.

"We're almost there," I assured her.

My hand was shaking at the thought of striking another human being—even Blanchard—but I was trying to convince myself I could do it to protect my sister and my friends. Suddenly, Blanchard stuck his hand in his sweatshirt pocket.

"Look out!" Mandy screamed. "He has another gun!"

*Whack! Whack!* Mandy and I each struck Blanchard on an ankle, and he yelped like a dog in double pain. What he dropped now wasn't a gun, but a small canister of mace like the mail carriers use to temporarily blind an attacking dog. I managed to grab the canister before it could roll over the edge.

"Now hold still!" I yelled. I was sweating like crazy now. Mandy and I had done what we had to do, but I really didn't want to hit the man again. I know in the movies they show the good guys looking all happy when they finally get the chance to harm or even kill their enemy. Well, Mandy and I were the good guys in this situation, but we definitely weren't feeling happy. All we wanted was for this nightmare to be over—to have Blanchard just stay put until we could hand him over to the police.

"They said it'll take at least twenty-five minutes to get out here," Aggie said when she and Alex returned to us. "The dispatcher lady thought we were nuts when I said we had Joe Blanchard out here and that he was trying to kill us. But they'll see."

"The funny thing is," Blanchard began saying between grunts of pain, "is that you still have no proof. I'm going to say that I saw you kids on the side of the road in the middle of the night and offered to take you home. Then you held me hostage and assaulted me with hammers. Just a crazy bunch of kids. No one will believe your story over mine." Blood dripped into the corner of his mouth and coated his teeth. He flashed a us a red, hideous smile.

Aggie pulled the tape recorder out of her purse and pressed the Rewind button for a couple of seconds. Then she pressed Play: "Just a crazy bunch of kids. No one will believe your story over mine," we heard Blanchard repeat.

"She's been recording the whole time we were down here," Alex said and patted his sister on the back.

Blanchard was stone silent now. He knew we had nailed him, thanks to Aggie. And, of course, we couldn't have done it without Bobby.

"Thank you, Bobby," I called out. "I think we can take it from here."

Blanchard suddenly crumpled to the floor with a thud. He arched his back against the shock isolator and winced, rubbing his ankles. And then I thought I heard the familiar *ka-chunk*, *ka-chunk* sound in the distance. I turned off the boombox and sure enough, there it was.

"You hear that?" I asked. "You guys go check!"

I held the mace canister in one hand and the hammer in the other, feeling confident that I could guard an injured man. The others dashed off to check the slifix.

"What's he saying?" I yelled.

"Oscar, foxtrot, foxtrot," Alex began calling out.

*Off?* I was thinking. *Off what?* I'm embarrassed to admit it, but I became so engrossed in trying to figure out what Bobby was saying that I took my eyes off my prisoner. Suddenly my legs were swept out from under me and I hit the floor hard on my tailbone. I managed to hold onto the mace, but the hammer joined the gun below the suspended floor of the capsule. Blanchard began limping out of the entryway toward the elevator. Maybe Mandy and I should have whacked him harder when we'd had the chance.

"Guys, help!" I screamed and got up. I was in pain, but I was more mad than hurt. As the twins got back to me, we heard the elevator door close. "I'm sorry," I said helplessly.

"Come on, the ladder!" Mandy shouted.

I stuck the mace in my pocket and ran out into the tunnel junction. I led the way up the ladder, sore tailbone and all. It was my fault that Blanchard had gotten away, so I felt it was my responsibility to get him back.

I pulled myself onto the topside platform just as the elevator door was scissoring open. I stood to the side and locked my arms out in front of me, aiming the canister as though it was a gun. Blanchard shuffled off the elevator and did a double-take when he saw me there.

"This is for Bobby," I said and sprayed. "*My* friend, not yours."

Man, that stuff really works! Blanchard dropped to the floor and sounded like he might cough up a lung. He was rubbing his eyes and wagging his head from side to side. The other twins and I started to cough too just from being in the area.

I opened the door to the security room and the four of us went in. Once we were breathing a little easier, Alex and I went back into the elevator vestibule to get our prisoner. We each grabbed an arm and led him to a chair in the security room where the girls were waiting with duct tape. We probably overdid it with the tape, using almost an entire roll to secure his arms, legs, and chest. But Blanchard had escaped once before and we wanted to make sure he was sitting there when the police arrived. I even put a piece of tape over his wound so it would stop grossing me out, and another piece over his mouth so he wouldn't have the chance to say anything. His voice was hateful to me.

Mandy and I went outside to roll open the gate when we finally heard a siren. The ground was soggy, but the rain had stopped. The two officers who responded to our call were baffled by the whole situation. We sat there in the security room and explained as much as we could. Aggie even played a portion of the recording for them while our prisoner sat there all taped up, with the exception of his mouth. The officers had pulled that piece from Blanchard's lips as soon as they arrived.

"Now wait a minute," Officer Clemm began. "You're telling us there's a ghost or a spirit downstairs?"

"Well, no. Probably not anymore," Alex said. "We think he left."

"I see," Officer Clemm responded suspiciously.

"These kids have a bad habit of making things up," Blanchard said and tried his best to weasel out of trouble. He told the officers that they shouldn't allow themselves to be taken in by a bunch of brats like us. And then, he even said that he was protected by something called diplomatic immunity because he was a U.S. congressman. "What that means, gentlemen, is that you're not even allowed to arrest me. It would actually be against the law for you to do it."

"This guy killed someone many years ago," I insisted. "And we're pretty sure he was gonna try to kill us right here, right now in a fire. We have that on tape too."

Officer Pearson went to the other side of the security room and spent a few minutes talking quietly on the phone. I mostly just heard him saying, "Mm-hm, mm-hm." When he came back to us he said to Blanchard, "Well, sir, our chief disagrees with you about the immunity business. Our orders are to cuff you and bring you in. Read him his rights, Jerry."

Blanchard didn't take advantage of his right to remain silent. The whole time that Officer Clemm was talking, the prisoner continually yelled things like, "This is an outrage," and "You'll wind up losing your badges because of this," and "You have no idea who you're messing with, do you?" Blanchard got himself so worked up that he was now as red as he had been while choking on the mace spray.

The two officers calmly cut him free from the tape and then handcuffed him. Blanchard glared at each of us as they led him out of the security room.

"See you in court," Alex called out to Blanchard. When we had Foxtrot-Zero all to ourselves again, Alex said, "Man, I've always wanted to say that!"

We all laughed and hugged, grateful to have made it through such a crazy ordeal. "We're a really good team!" Mandy said.

"A *great* team!" I added.

And just then, Aggie's cell phone rang. "Uh-oh!" she said and answered. We could hear poor Ms. Burke screaming, wondering where in the world we were at four o'clock in the morning. Aggie didn't lie; she told her mother we had gone to Foxtrot-Zero for something incredibly important.

"Okay. I know, Mom. I'm really sorry," Aggie was saying. She bit her lip. "Okay. I understand. I know. We're all sorry."

"Well?" I said when the phone conversation was over.

"Not good," Aggie sighed. "Mom got up to use the bathroom and just happened to check in on us. She freaked. She's calling your parents at the hotel and they're all gonna come screaming out here."

"Oh boy," Mandy said. "This should be interesting. We're probably all grounded until we're eighteen."

"No matter what, it was worth it," I said. "We got Blanchard and we helped our friend."

"Hey, we never finished reading his message!" Mandy reminded us.

I held Aggie's hand as we entered the elevator vestibule.

# CHAPTER FIFTEEN

Now that the capsule wasn't haunted anymore it seemed eerier than ever. I know that sounds weird, but it's true. It's like you could feel in the air that something—or rather, some*one*—was missing, and even the electrical hum seemed to be asking where Bobby was. The final message he left for us on the slifix read as follows:

OSCAR FOXTROT FOXTROT
TANGO OSCAR
JULIETT FOXTROT

TANGO
TANGO

I pressed the form-feed button and tore off the message. We set it on the commander's console and tried to make sense of it.

"Off to JF," we all said.

"I get it!" Mandy cried. "He's off to find Jennifer Franklin!"

"All right, Bobby!" I cheered.

"What about the two T's at the end?" Alex asked.

"Tango is 'thank you' in military talk," I said. "Our dad still uses that sometime. Bobby's saying 'Thank you, thank you' to us at the end."

"Go Bobby, go Bobby!" we started chanting and pumping our fists in the air.

I knew we would go ahead with our plan for a memorial marker at Foxtrot-Zero, but I suddenly got an idea for another tribute to our friend Bobby—a tribute we could offer right at that moment. While my fellow twins continued the "Bobby" chant, I went over to the boombox and cued up the Beach Boys' "A Young Man Is Gone."

I tapped Aggie on the shoulder and held my arms open. "May I?" I asked, like I'd heard men do in the dancehall scenes of old movies. Aggie smiled and embraced me. My head was at her shoulder level, so we must have looked like an awkward couple. That didn't matter to me, though. Then Mandy and Boy Genius followed our lead. My eyes met Mandy's for a moment and we smiled at each other. I knew I couldn't ask for a better sister.

My slow dance with Aggie at Foxtrot-Zero felt like a soothing dream, and I didn't want it to end. I couldn't believe I had resisted the idea of coming out to North Dakota in the first place. I realized that in the short time we were there, I had grown a lot—like a sunflower—at least on the inside. As it turns out, you never know what life has waiting for you just around the corner. I held Aggie a little tighter, closed my eyes, and let the music wash over me:

> Now a young man is gone
> But his legend lingers on
> For so much had he to give . . .

*The End*

# SNEAK PEEK:
## DOUBLE-TWINS MYSTERY #2

One year has passed since the Cousineau twins of Ohio and the Burke twins of North Dakota teamed up to solve the mystery of Bobby Swenson's death. Now, on the brink of the Burkes' visit to Cleveland, the kids experience some strange coincidences: Birds land on Mark and Aggie at precisely the same moment, even though they're separated by over 1,000 miles; and Mandy and Alex independently find the same out-of-print mystery in used book stores and stop reading on the exact same page.

"These are the kinds of signs I've been waiting for!" Alex exclaims during a video chat. "Signs that the four of us have more work to do." As usual, Alex is right.

The sudden death of 91-year-old Arabella Hoffer is accepted by her Cleveland family and friends as a natural event, but the Double-Twins know better. They know because Arabella herself is apparently sending them clues from beyond the grave in a most unusual fashion! The twins must draw on their individual talents and collective courage to discover who murdered the kindhearted, passionate lady that they've come to think of as Aunt Arabella.

*Off the Wall,* the second novel in the Double-Twins Mystery Series, is scheduled for release in early 2016.

# ABOUT THE AUTHOR

Paul Kijinski is the author of the novel *Camp Limestone*, winner of a 2007 Paterson Prize for Books for Young Readers, and other works of middle grade fiction. *The 11:15 Bench*, published in 2013, is a novel for adult readers.

Kijinski was born in Garfield Heights, Ohio, and earned degrees from Oberlin College, The Ohio State University, and John Carroll University. He began writing seriously while serving as a missile officer in the U.S. Air Force. The solitude of underground launch control centers provided a uniquely rich environment for putting pen to paper. His final assignment in the military was teaching English at the Air Force Academy.

Kijinski is currently an elementary school teacher in South Euclid, Ohio. He and his wife, Eileen, have two adult sons.

You may follow him on Facebook.

23928450R00094

Made in the USA
Middletown, DE
08 September 2015